THE MYSTERIOUS HIDEAWAY

Adventures
of the Northwoods

THE
MYSTERIOUS
HIDEAWAY

Lois Walfrid Johnson

BETHANY HOUSE PUBLISHERS
MINNEAPOLIS, MINNESOTA 55438

Caleb Greene, miller at the Hickerson Roller Mill, helped with the research of Dr. Harvey Wiley, author of the 1906 Pure Food and Drugs Act. Big Gust Anderson, Grantsburg's village marshall, Charlie Saunders, Burnett County sheriff, and August Cassel, the auctioneer, lived in northwest Wisconsin during the early 1900s. Mr. Peters is based on the historic Peter Schyttner. All other characters in this book are fictitious. Any resemblance to persons living or dead is coincidental.

Cover illustration by Andrea Jorgenson.

Published by Bethany House Publishers
A Ministry of Bethany Fellowship, Inc.
6820 Auto Club Road, Minneapolis, Minnesota 55438

Printed in the United States of America

Library of Congress Cataloging-in-Publication Data

Johnson, Lois Walfrid.
    The mysterious hideaway / Lois Walfrid Johnson.
        p.   cm. — (Adventures of the northwoods : bk. 6)
    Summary: Kate, Anders, and Erik investigate baffling clues that lead them to tunnels in the woodpile, stolen food, and a hidden ladder.

    [1. Swedish Americans—Fiction.] 2. Mystery and detective stories.
3. Christian life—Fiction.] I. Title. II. Series: Johnson, Lois Walfrid. Adventures of the northwoods ; 6.
PZ7.J63255My   1992
[Fic]—dc20   92–13903
                                                        CIP
ISBN 1–55661–238–9   AC

To Kevin and Lyn,
Nate and Karin

with my prayer
that you will reach high for your dreams,
always keeping God at the center.

LOIS WALFRID JOHNSON is the author of *Just A Minute, Lord*, *You're My Best Friend, Lord*, and such adult books as *Gift in My Arms* for new mothers. *You're Worth More Than You Think!* and other books in her Let's-Talk-About-It Stories for Kids Series helps preteens make wise choices.

Lois' work has received many awards, including the Gold Medallion and the Laura Ingalls Wilder Award. Yet there's something she values even more—knowing her work has been helpful in the lives of readers. She and her husband, Roy, who plays a supportive role in her writing, are the parents of three married children and live in rural Wisconsin.

Contents

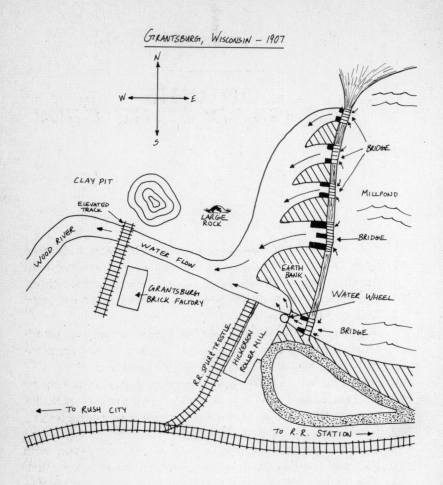

GRANTSBURG, WISCONSIN - 1907

N
W — E
S

CLAY PIT

ELEVATED TRACK

LARGE ROCK

WOOD RIVER

WATER FLOW

GRANTSBURG BRICK FACTORY

BRIDGE

MILLPOND

BRIDGE

EARTH BANK

WATER WHEEL

BRIDGE

R.R. SPUR & TRESTLE

HICKERON ROLLER MILL

← TO RUSH CITY

TO R.R. STATION →

1

The Disappearing Face

*W*hen the wagon rolled to a stop, Katherine O'Connell jumped to the ground. Her long black hair shone in the midday sunlight. Her deep blue eyes sparkled with laughter.

"Just because it's April Fools' Day, you think you'll catch me on something! Well, you won't!"

Kate's stepbrother Anders winked at their friend Erik Lundgren. When Erik grinned, Kate knew for sure. They were planning something. Well, they wouldn't get by with it!

Kate crossed the circle drive, then turned back to look at the huge building where they'd stopped. HICKERSON ROLLER MILL was sprawled across the front in three-foot-high letters, followed by SNOW FLAKE FLOUR.

On this warm and sunny day, the mill was a busy place with wagons from the surrounding countryside. Beneath a low shed-like roof, Erik and Anders unloaded sacks of grain onto a platform. When they finished, Erik drove the horses away from the building.

As he and Kate walked back to the main entry, she kept looking up. Five stories high, the Hickerson Mill was the tallest building for miles around. Far above the shed-like roof was a small window.

Just then a man with a triangular-shaped face appeared in the opening. Wide at the forehead, his face tapered down to a narrow chin.

Kate grabbed Erik's arm. "Did you see that?"

"See what?" Erik asked.

"That face." Kate pointed. "There's a man looking out of that window."

But when Anders and Erik looked up where Kate was staring, the face was gone.

"Aw, Kate," Anders complained, "that's the oldest April Fools' trick in the book."

Kate flipped her long braid over her shoulder. "I'm not trying to fool you. Someone was there, watching us."

"Sure, sure," said Anders. "Nothing up there but bins for storing grain."

"I tell you, I saw someone," Kate insisted.

Neither of the boys listened to her. Like Anders, Erik was six feet tall and broad-shouldered from farm work. But Erik's hair was wavy and brown, while Anders had a thatch of blond hair that fell this way and that.

Anders slung a heavy sack of oats across his broad shoulder. Erik picked up a second sack, and Kate followed them through an open door. Just inside, men were putting their grain on a scale set in the floor.

Erik and Anders dropped their sacks off to one side and went back for more. During that first week of April 1907, it seemed that every farmer in northwest Wisconsin had come into the village of Grantsburg. All of them needed their oats cleaned and ready for spring planting.

"It'll be a while, boys," said the man at the scale. "Why don't you leave your oats and come back? I'll take yours in turn."

When the man finished weighing a sack, he poured the grain into an opening next to the scale. Small cups mounted on a belt lifted the oats through a wooden chute. On the floor above, a fanning mill cleaned weed seeds and other debris from the oats.

As Anders and Erik carried the rest of their sacks from the wagon, Kate started exploring. A year ago her mother had married Anders' father, Carl Nordstrom. Mama and Kate had moved from Minneapolis to Windy Hill Farm. Since that time, Kate had never had an opportunity to visit the mill.

Passing chutes and wide belts that led to the floor above or the floor below, Kate walked to the doorway of a room filled with big machines. The man who worked there told Kate they were roller mills. As grains of wheat passed through the mills, rollers opened the kernels to make Snow Flake flour.

Beyond the large machines on the other side of the room, windows were thrown open to the warm and sunny day. When Kate crossed over to them, she found they overlooked the Wood River.

Far below, a series of dams held back water to make a millpond. Now, in spring, high water spilled over four of these dams, creating waterfalls. A powerful fifth stream flowed alongside the mill.

From somewhere beneath the floor came a deep rumble. As Kate turned from the windows, the worker pulled up a trapdoor that opened into the ground below. Beneath them lay a huge wheel on its side. Swiftly moving water poured into the mill, struck the wheel, spun it around, then flowed back into the river.

"That's our power," the man said. "The wheel makes everything else go."

Kate listened to the roar of water and watched its spray for a few minutes. But her thoughts kept returning to the man in the window. There was something about his face that she couldn't forget. What was it?

Still feeling curious, Kate decided to keep exploring. Soon she found a stairway leading to the next floor.

As she started up the steps, Erik joined her. "Let's take a look around," he said.

Kate stopped. Erik was her special friend, but she'd rather search by herself. If there was nothing there, he wouldn't be able to tease her.

"So you believe me now?" she asked. "Do you think there's someone there? Someone who shouldn't be, I mean?"

"Wellll—" Erik didn't seem convinced. "It won't hurt to

look." He let Kate lead him toward the stairs.

Partway to the floor above, Kate stopped. What if there really was a man somewhere near? She didn't have any idea who he was or why he was lurking around the building. Suddenly she didn't feel so eager to go first.

When Erik caught up, a teasing sparkle lit his eyes. "Curious Kate, that's what Anders will call you."

Kate raised her chin. "I tell you, I saw someone up there."

Erik laughed. "Yah, sure. But we'll get a good view from the window."

At the top of the steps an open area led off in three directions. Directly ahead were large bins for storing grain. Six or eight feet wide, the bins looked like tall wooden boxes that stretched from the floor almost to the ceiling.

Next to the closest bin was a ladder made of boards nailed to the wall. Erik started up to a narrow catwalk. "C'mon, Kate," he called.

But Kate was already pushing back the small door at the bottom of a bin. The bin was empty, with only a scattering of grain where wheat had been stored.

When she went on to the next bin, she found it full, with the door held down by grain pushing against it. A narrow passageway led off to still other storage places.

Instead of following the passageway, Kate went over to a window bright with sunlight. Some distance below were the wagons, and beyond that a railroad track leading into the main streets of Grantsburg. While coming into town, Kate had heard the whistle for the noon train.

Now she wondered, *Is this the place where the man stood?* It was the right side of the building. Yet from below, the window seemed farther from the ground.

Once more, Kate moved into the dim passageway between tall bins. As Erik followed her through the semidarkness, Kate heard a muffled sound.

She paused, her heart racing. Had something moved?

Suddenly a gray cat leaped out of the shadows. As he streaked past Kate, she jumped.

Erik laughed. "Spooks got you, Kate?"

Kate straightened her shoulders. Not for anything would she let Erik think she was afraid. But as she passed a second, then a third bin, a shadow slid across the opening ahead of her.

Again Kate stopped. Her feet felt nailed to the floor. Erik stumbled into her.

"What's the matter?" he asked.

Without speaking, Kate peered ahead. *I imagined it*, she thought. Yet as she stood without moving, she seemed to hear another sound—feet running across the wood floor.

A chill chased down Kate's spine. *There's someone here, after all*. Again she thought of the man who had stared out the window.

"Let's keep looking." Erik sounded impatient.

Kate dreaded the thought of going on. Still, if she didn't, Erik would call her a scaredy-cat.

Quickly Kate hurried through the narrow walkway and came to a large room. In the doorway she paused to look around.

On the far side of the room was a large square hole. A railing surrounded the hole to protect people from tumbling into the floor below.

Far above, a rope hung from a wooden pulley in the ceiling. The longest end of the rope was stretched tight, tied to a post on the ground floor. The other end of the rope hung over the railing, ready for men to lift machinery or boxes from the floor below.

The room seemed to be used for storing different kinds of equipment. Light from a dust-covered window fell on some large iron pieces. In other places shadows darkened everything along the wall.

Next to where Kate stood, a tall cupboard reached far above her head. Still feeling uneasy, she edged away. Was there someone hiding in the shadows?

Trying to push aside her fear, Kate started past the cupboard. Too late she sensed a quick movement from the other side. Someone grabbed her arms from behind.

"Help!" Kate cried, fighting against the hands that held her.

Two voices shouted in unison, "April fool!"

Erik and Anders!

"You meanies!" Kate sputtered.

Anders laughed. When he dropped his hold, Kate sagged with relief.

The next instant anger filled every part of her being. Twisting, she pounded her fists against her brother's chest. "How did you get here?"

A lopsided grin lit his face. "I snuck up the steps when you were looking at the water wheel."

"How could you do this to me?" Kate stormed. "You are the most awful boys in the whole world!"

As she trembled, Anders laughed. "Pretty good joke, huh?"

But Erik looked from Kate to Anders. "Maybe not so good. She really got scared."

He stretched out a hand. "C'mon, Kate. Let's go downstairs."

Unwilling to accept Erik's help when he'd been so mean, Kate stepped back. As she edged toward the window, she looked beyond him. In the light that came through the hole in the floor, she saw that something had changed.

The end of the long rope no longer hung over the railing. Now, as it dangled from the ceiling to the ground floor, it swung back and forth.

2

High Water

$\mathcal{K}$ate stared. Who had taken the rope from the railing? Only one thing could cause its mysterious movement.

Darting forward, she looked down into the room below. Light shone through a large window, but she could see no one.

She had been so close to finding the man! While the boys scared her, he had seen his chance.

"He got away!" she exclaimed.

"Who got away?" Anders asked.

"The man who looked from the window. He slipped out of the shadows and slid down the rope."

Anders groaned. "Kate, you've got too big an imagination."

"It's not my imagination. I saw him in the window. Gray hair. Starting to lose it in front. Lines in his forehead. His face looked like a triangle."

"A triangle?" This time it was Erik who laughed.

Kate nodded. "A wide forehead and a narrow chin. A triangle."

Anders hooted. "And what color eyes did he have?"

"I couldn't see from that distance." Kate walked over to one of the windows. Just below was the roof that covered the entry-way at the front of the building.

"This isn't the window," Kate said. The angle for looking up from below would be wrong. "The man was higher. Come on, I'll find it."

Quickly she walked between the tall bins to the stairway. Partway up the flight of steps, she came to a window overlooking the large storage shed. A railroad spur, or short track, led off the main one. Freight cars stood there, with men unloading corn or wheat from the Dakotas and Minnesota.

Kate continued up another flight. When she reached the top floor, she stood still for a moment, looking around. Large pulleys held wide reinforced canvas belts that came up through the floor. Here and there, boards were nailed to studs in the wall, provid-ing ladders for men to fix the belts if needed.

A walkway led to the back of the building and windows above the river. But Kate was most interested in the single window that faced the front side.

She started toward it, then saw holes in the floor. Loose boards crossed the heavy support beams. Some of the boards looked thin and old, flimsy at best. Light from the floor below shone between them.

Kate stopped. Though she was short and light, the boards might not hold her weight.

When Erik came up behind her, she turned. "How could someone get to that window?"

Erik shook his head. "There's no way a man could cross those boards. He'd fall through to the floor below."

"Only a fool would try it," Anders said. "The boards are dry. They'd crack under a man's weight."

"Even a small man?" Kate asked.

Erik nodded, as though hating to disappoint her. "Even a small man."

"But I saw him!" Kate insisted.

"Sure, Kate, sure." Clearly Anders did not believe her.

Kate stared at the boards, still trying to see a way to the window.

Anders started toward the stairs. "I'm hungry," he said. "It's past lunch."

But Kate called him back. "Look!" She pointed. "Footprints!"

On the dusty floorboards, the footprints turned slightly, as though the person tested each board before stepping on it. In the dim light a path wound this way and that to the window.

Erik whistled. "Somehow he always managed to step on a support beam instead of just a board. You were right!"

"Yah, little sister," Anders drawled. "Have to hand it to you. But what does it prove? A man looked out the window. So what? It could be any man—like a farmer who decided to look around."

Kate shook her head. "I don't think so."

"I don't think so either." Erik was still staring at the footprints. "I think it's someone who's a carpenter."

Instantly Kate saw what he meant. Her Daddy O'Connell had been a carpenter. As a small child she'd watched him walk across partly finished buildings, always seeming to know where to step. Daddy had died in a construction accident, but it had nothing to do with his understanding of safety in high places.

Even now, two years after the accident, Kate felt an ache of loneliness whenever she thought about her father. She swallowed around the tightness in her throat.

"I think Erik's right—that the man was a carpenter," she said. "Whoever he is, he's probably short and doesn't weigh much."

Anders pointed. "With feet that are small for a man."

Kate glanced down at her brother's big feet. "Yah, sure," she teased, saying the words the way Anders would. He was wearing his father's old boots. Papa Nordstrom had given them to Anders when he grew out of everything he owned.

"Well, I'm still hungry," Anders said.

Kate followed him to the steps, but kept looking around. "I wouldn't want to be lost in here on a dark night."

As they reached the ground floor, a train whistle shrieked. A moment later, the Blueberry Special rumbled by on its way out of town.

The man operating the large scale had just finished weighing their last sack of oats. "There you are," he said. "And there's the flour for your mother." He pointed to a cloth bag set a bit apart from the others.

Anders and Erik carried the sacks one by one out to the wagon. When they finished loading, Erik pulled a heavy blanket over the grain, then a canvas over that.

When Anders picked up the lunch basket, Lutfisk leaped to his feet. Named *Lute fisk* after the dried cod Swedes eat at Christmas, the dog belonged to Anders. As Kate and the boys started toward the millpond, Lutfisk bounded alongside.

Bridges without railings formed a walkway above the five dams. Kate stopped on the first bridge and watched as the water rushed beneath her, then swooshed into the building to where the large wheel would be. Farther on, at a right angle to where it flowed in, water poured back out into the river.

Next came a large bank of earth, then the other four dams for raising and lowering the water level of the pond. Now, in spring, the Wood River tumbled over those dams, creating waterfalls.

"Let's go to the clay pit," Anders called as he started across the second bridge.

Farther down the river, on the same side as the mill, lay the Grantsburg Brick Factory. An elevated track crossed the water, ending at a huge hole in the ground. When Anders headed in that direction, Kate and Erik followed.

The pit formed a large circle with steep sides dropping to a depth of almost seventy feet. Only where Kate stood did the ground slant away more gradually.

Nearby, Anders found a large rock and sat down to watch men dig clay from the pit. As Kate took out the food, she saw what looked like ore cars carrying clay to the factory.

Anders was feeding Lutfisk a sandwich when Kate glanced back toward the mill. A high railroad trestle ran along this end of the building.

"Why does Mama want her wheat ground into flour here?" she asked. "Aren't there mills closer to home?"

"Caleb Greene is the miller here," Anders said, as if that explained everything. He made it sound as if Mr. Greene were the most important person in the world.

"Mr. Greene doesn't use anything artificial to whiten the flour," Erik added. "He works with Dr. Wiley."

"Who's that?"

"Harvey Wiley. The head chemist for the Department of Agriculture. He used Mr. Greene's flour for research. Last year Mr. Wiley got the Pure Food and Drugs Act through Congress."

As Kate bit into her sandwich, Anders stretched out his long legs. "Right now, my dear sister, you are eating Snow Flake flour! That's the only flour Mama will use to make bread."

Just then Kate saw a short, slender man come out of a door onto the trestle. For a moment he stood in the sunlight, looking around. Beneath gray hair and a high forehead was a triangular-shaped face.

"Look!" Kate whispered, turning to Erik. "It's the man I saw!"

Quickly Erik looked toward the mill.

But when Kate turned back the man was gone. Even the shadowed space beneath the heavy trestle seemed empty.

"Aw, Kate!" Anders exclaimed. "What's the matter with you? You're getting strange!"

"I'm not! I saw that man again. You did, too, didn't you, Erik?"

"Yup! Right near that freight car that's unloading wheat."

"See, Anders? Erik saw him too."

Anders leaned back against the rock. "That so? Tell me how he looked, my good friend."

Erik grinned. "Well, he was tall and fat, and he had big muscular arms. He looked ready to pounce on a short little girl named Kate."

"You're making things up!"

Erik caught her hand. A spark of laughter lit his eyes. Yet beneath his teasing, Kate glimpsed a streak of kindness.

"When I looked, there was no one there," he said now. Always Erik seemed to care about what happened to her.

"But you saw the footprints in the mill!"

Erik nodded. "Sure, we saw 'em, but—" He broke off, as if not wanting to discourage Kate more.

"Those footprints could have been made by anyone at any time in the last few weeks," said Anders.

Kate bit her lip. She knew her brother was right, and there was nothing she could say to change his mind.

Just the same, she quickly gathered up the remaining sandwiches and dropped them into the basket. "Let's go look."

Anders groaned. "Why do I have to have a sister like you?" Reaching out, he snatched another sandwich. "Curious Kate!"

Unwilling to waste any more time, Kate picked up the big basket. Anders followed, still eating his sandwich.

Near the walkway over the river, he found a stick and showed it to Lutfisk. Partway across the second bridge, Anders threw the stick into the millpond. "Go get it!" he commanded.

Lutfisk leaped off the bridge. Water sprayed up, then settled, as the dog paddled toward the floating stick. Grasping it in his mouth, he turned and started back toward Anders.

"Good boy!" Anders shouted.

Just then the current caught the dog. He fought hard, trying to make it to shore. But the force of the water funneled him straight toward the bridge.

Kate caught one glimpse of the terror in her brother's face. Then Lutfisk tumbled over the dam.

3

Another Discovery!

*A*s Kate scrambled to the other side of the bridge, she saw the dog. Just beyond the dam, his body spun round and round with the force of the current.

First Anders, then Erik leaped off the bridge onto a bank of earth. Still tumbling, the dog swept past them. His brown and black body appeared, then disappeared, washing downstream.

Anders stumbled across the uneven ground, trying to catch up. Once the dog's head appeared above water. The next moment it vanished again.

Where the stream joined the main part of the river, Anders caught up. As the current washed Lutfisk into shallow water, Anders grabbed him. Clutching the dog to his chest, he waded to shore.

From where Kate stood, Lutfisk looked limp and lifeless. With tears in her eyes, Kate watched Anders and Erik bend over him. What could be worse than for Anders to lose his dog?

Then Lutfisk moved. Anders loosened his hold, and the dog struggled out of his arms. On wobbly legs, Lutfisk stood up.

Anders looked as though he couldn't believe it. He threw his arms around the dog and hugged him. "I'm sorry, I'm sorry," he kept repeating over and over.

Lutfisk reached out his tongue and licked his master's face.

Anders groaned. "How could I do that to you? Throwing the stick too close to the dam!"

Gently he picked up the dog and carried him up the steep bank. Erik helped Anders lift him onto the bridge.

For a moment the dog stood there, looking dazed. Then he shook himself. Water sprayed in all directions. Yet Kate had never felt so glad to get wet.

As they started back to the mill, Lutfisk padded alongside Anders. The tall blond boy watched the dog closely. He walked normally, and Anders looked relieved.

When they reached Lundgren's farm wagon, Erik set the basket of food in the spot he'd saved just behind the seat. Kate looked around.

With her worry about Lutfisk, she'd almost forgotten the strange little man. Now she saw no sign of him and felt sure he would either be gone or well hidden.

Anders was wet to his knees. "Good thing it's such a warm day!" he said as he wrung out the bottom of his overall legs. "We'll dry out fast."

While Erik untied the horses, Kate settled herself on the wagon seat. With Lutfisk in his arms, Anders climbed up beside her.

Erik clucked to Queen and Prince. As they entered the road past the mill, they met another team of horses. A newly born colt ran alongside its mother, but Anders didn't even notice. Starting at Lutfisk's head and working down the spine, he felt the dog, still checking for something wrong.

"I can't believe I did that." Anders shook his head, as though hating to even think what might have happened.

"It's a miracle he's all right," Kate said. She still felt shaky about it.

Twisting around, she reached into the basket to rescue her half-eaten sandwich. The sacks of oats made large humps under the canvas.

Erik turned the wagon toward the center of Grantsburg. Kate finished her sandwich and leaned down for another half. Just then the canvas that covered the grain sacks seemed to move. Kate stared at the canvas, then decided they'd ridden over a bump.

When they reached the main street, Erik stopped the horses at a hitching post.

"Got a treat for you, Kate." Anders wore his lopsided grin, as though glad to think about something besides the near drowning. "Papa said we could get ice cream."

Anders lifted Lutfisk onto the wagon seat, then climbed down. Kate hurried into Unseth's drugstore after her brother and Erik.

Along one wall was a high marble-topped counter. Behind that were kegs of ice cream, kept cold with ice.

When Kate told the man what she wanted, he gave her two big scoops of vanilla. Holding her dish as if it were a treasure, Kate carried it over to a small table. With her mouth watering, she sat down on a wire-backed chair.

Kate popped a spoonful into her mouth. "Ummmmm," she said as the boys joined her. She moved her tongue around the ice cream, wanting to savor the treat as long as possible. When it slipped down her throat, she ate the next mouthful even more slowly.

Nearby, a mother and young girl sat at another table. When the little girl smiled, she reminded Kate of her five-year-old sister Tina. Kate wished she could bring ice cream back for her.

In the corner of the room, a heavyset man sat with a very large dish in front of him. His brown hair was neatly trimmed, but mud from his boots dirtied the floor.

As Kate continued eating, she forgot about him. Right now the special treat seemed the most important thing in the world.

Anders seemed to enjoy the taste just as much. He was slurping ice cream off his spoon when Big Gust, Grantsburg's village marshall, walked in.

"Anders!" Gust exclaimed in his deep voice. "Kate!" Only a few days before, the marshall had helped them with a mystery involving a timber swindler. Now the gentle giant stretched out his hand, welcoming them back to town.

When Anders stood to offer his hand, the man in the corner looked up. His gaze traveled from the top of the marshall's seven-foot six-inch-tall body, to the star on his chest, then to his size eighteen boots.

Suddenly the man pushed back the dish still filled with ice cream and stood up. As he crossed to the door, he coughed from deep in his chest. Outside, he clumped across the wooden sidewalk.

Through the window, Kate saw him climb into a high-wheeled buggy with wooden spokes.

"Have you seen that stranger around before?" Big Gust asked the man scooping ice cream. "Looks like he's feeling guilty about something."

When the man behind the counter shook his head, Gust watched the buggy roll down the street. "I think I'll keep an eye on him."

———

When Anders, Erik, and Kate left the drugstore, Lutfisk was nowhere in sight. Anders whistled, and the dog came running. "Well, he's back to normal!" Again Anders looked relieved.

On the ride home deep ruts filled the road, often widening into large holes. As the horses strained forward in the harness, their hooves sank down into spring mud.

The soft ground reminded Kate of the baseball game the day before. In spite of a wet field, the Trade Lake team had played.

"Wasn't that a good game yesterday?" she asked.

Anders grinned. "Can't get much closer than 6 to 5. It's all right as long as we won."

"Pretty soon we can play at school," Kate said slyly.

"*We?*" asked her brother. "Did you say *we* can play?"

"Yup!" Kate tossed her long braid over her shoulder. "You and Erik and Lars are glad to let me play when I field for you at home."

"That's different."

"Why? You know I'm a good player."

"Hah!"

"You're just afraid I'll beat you!"

Anders snorted, as though that was too dumb an idea to even consider.

For some time the three rode in silence. More than once, as muddy water splattered, Kate glanced back to make sure the oats and flour were covered.

Each time a wheel bounced down into a hole, the wagon shuddered. As Kate clutched the edge of the seat, the eleven miles to the farm stretched out forever.

By the time they reached the mailbox, red and gold colored the western sky. In the last rays of light Anders jumped down for their newspaper. When he climbed aboard again, Erik did not need to urge the horses off the main road. They knew they were headed home.

As the long dirt road wound between trees, Queen and Prince picked up speed and Lutfisk disappeared, chasing a squirrel. Before long, the wagon entered into a pasture dotted with stumps. Then the log barn of Windy Hill Farm rose up on their left.

Almost immediately afterward, another building loomed up on their right. In the dusk the granary clung to the side of the hill. Erik stopped the wagon in front of it.

The boys went inside, and Kate climbed down and walked around one end of the building. On clear days she loved this view across Rice Lake to the distant horizon. Now only a line of red remained in the western sky. Far above, a star shone brightly.

Soon Anders and Erik returned and carried one sack after another into the granary. On both floors were large bins for storing grain.

When only the Lundgren oats were left in the wagon, Anders shouldered the bag of flour. Erik's horses trotted off toward home. Kate and Anders walked together to the Windy Hill farmhouse.

Later Kate was to remember that peaceful walk when she tried to think back, putting together the events of that night.

———

As Anders and Kate entered the kitchen, the fragrant smell of warm bread reached them. With a running jump, Tina leaped into Kate's arms. Wisps of white-blond hair escaped the little girl's pigtails, curling around her face.

From the kitchen table redheaded Lars grinned his welcome. Beneath his freckles, he still looked pale from his bout with pneumonia.

Beyond Lars, Papa Nordstrom stood at the wood cookstove. Kate smiled at the unusual sight of her stepfather with a large pot of stew. But Papa didn't seem to mind. Even as he stirred, he glanced toward Mama, sitting in her chair near the window.

In the lamplight Mama's hair seemed even more golden than usual. Slowly she rocked back and forth, cradling the newest Nordstrom, born only three days before.

As soon as Kate washed her hands, she hurried over to the baby. His body was snugly wrapped in a flannel blanket, and his tiny eyes closed in sleep. Thick blond hair covered his head.

Bernhard Carl, thought Kate. The baby was named after her stepfather, Carl, and her uncle Ben, whose real name was Bernhard.

"Can I hold him?" she asked, and Mama held up the small bundle. Taking her place in the chair, Kate leaned back, rocking the baby.

Surprise still filled Kate each time she felt how light he was. As she pulled aside the blanket, Bernie opened his eyes and looked up. His head moved as though he were searching for her face.

Gently Kate grasped Bernie's little hand. When she placed her finger against his palm, his tiny fingers closed around hers.

Just then Mama's brother Ben came in from outside. As the wind caught the door, it slammed shut. The baby jumped, then let out a frightened cry.

"Ben!" Kate exclaimed. "You scared him!"

"I'm sorry," he said.

Gathering the little one to her, Kate held him up and patted his back until he quieted.

As soon as Ben shed his coat, he came over. From his six-foot three-inch-tall height he looked down.

Kate turned Bernie for Ben to see. He still seemed unable to believe that Mama and Papa had named the baby after him.

When the family gathered around the table for supper, Kate cradled Bernie in her left arm. By the time Papa finished the table prayer, the baby's eyes were closed.

A little longer Kate held him, shifting him so she could watch him sleep. For many months she had hoped the baby would be a sister.

"Think he can play baseball in another week?" Anders asked. He'd gotten what he wanted—a boy—and he'd probably never let Kate forget.

Standing up, Kate offered the baby to him.

Anders edged away. "Just waiting for him to grow another inch."

But Kate knew Anders felt uncomfortable about holding a creature so small. When Bernie grew older, it would make more of a difference that he was a boy. Right now he was a baby Kate could enjoy.

While eating, she and Anders told about their day, but neither of them mentioned the disappearing face. Then Mama encouraged Ben to start school when spring term opened in a week.

Ben spoke English surprisingly well for being in America only six months, but he didn't know how to read and write his new language.

"I will be old," he said.

"Old for going to school?" Anders asked. "Nah, you're Miss Sundquist's age."

"The teacher? She will like that I go to class?"

Anders grinned. "She will like it. You can sit next to me."

Kate coughed. It wasn't hard to guess what would happen then. Anders could stir up plenty of trouble.

"I think you should go, Ben—at least till spring planting starts." Above his neatly trimmed beard, Papa's face was weathered from working outside. "It's still too wet to work in the fields."

After supper, Papa pushed back his chair and opened the

newspaper. As Kate gathered up the dishes, she looked over his shoulder.

In the lamplight she read the headline: TRUSTED EM-PLOYEE STEALS VALUABLE COINS. Below that was a picture.

As Kate recognized the face, she gasped. "That's the man I saw in the mill!"

4

The Mysterious Woodpile

*A*nders hurried around the table. Standing in back of Papa, he looked down at the newspaper. "You're sure?" he asked Kate.

"Of course, I'm sure. See his face? Broad in the forehead, and a narrow chin?"

"What's it say?" Anders asked. As the family gathered around, Papa read aloud:

"A Minneapolis family has reported their shock and dismay about the betrayal of a trusted family servant. Mr. and Mrs. Stanley Kempe told police that Thomas Evans, a man who served them faithfully for over 15 years, stole several valuable coins from a hidden safe in the house.

"Only three people knew about the safe—Mr. and Mrs. Kempe and Thomas Evans, who installed the safe a year ago. Shortly after Mrs. Kempe talked with Mr. Evans about the theft, he disappeared, adding to suspicions about his guilt.

" 'Mr. Evans was a careful carpenter and able to do anything we asked around the house,' said Mr. Kempe in a statement to the newspaper. 'We trusted him as we trusted no one else. We are deeply disappointed.'

"The couple described the man as having gray hair, a receding hairline, and black eyes. He is short and thin and walks with a slight stoop in his shoulders."

"You *saw* the man?" Mama asked Kate when Papa finished reading.

Kate nodded. "Both the picture and the description fit."

Mama's wide blue eyes looked troubled. "I don't like the idea of someone like that running around the woods."

"I saw him in Grantsburg," Kate said quickly. "Not here."

She tossed her braid over her shoulder and grinned. "Anders didn't see him at all. He thought I was making things up."

Anders leaned back in his chair. "Well, you know, Kate's imagination and all." He winked at Papa. "Somehow she always manages to see something."

But Papa didn't think it was funny. "Tell me everything you noticed," he said to Kate.

When she finished telling about the mysterious man, Papa asked her to go back over some of the details. Finally he nodded. "I'll go in and talk to Charlie Saunders tomorrow. As sheriff, he should know about this."

———

The next evening Papa returned from Grantsburg with the news that neither Charlie nor Big Gust had seen a trace of Thomas Evans. Two days slipped by with no one learning anything more.

During the week the weather turned cold again. When the sharp wind gusted across an open field, Kate felt as if they'd returned to winter.

On Friday Papa and Anders and Ben split firewood. Papa had the contract to keep the Spirit Lake School supplied. When spring term started Monday, the students would need a fire to stay warm.

The next morning Papa asked Anders to haul a wagon load. As her brother hitched up Dolly and Florie, the family's large workhorses, Kate decided to go along.

When they reached the schoolhouse, Anders directed the

horses around to the woodshed. About sixteen feet long, the shed was painted red. On one end was the boys' outhouse, on the other end the outhouse for the girls. Behind the shed, the hill sloped away to a creek.

Anders and Kate climbed down to unload the wagon. The side of the shed closest to the school had large double doors. When Anders swung them open, Kate saw a high row of neatly stacked wood.

Anders pushed back his cap and scratched his head. "Something's wrong," he said. "There shouldn't be this much wood."

"That's a problem?" Kate asked. "Sounds good to me."

"See how high it's stacked in front? It wasn't that way when we got out of school at Christmas."

Stepping forward, Anders stood on tiptoe, gazing over the front row. "That's odd!" he exclaimed.

Still looking puzzled, Anders pushed the doors farther open. When he spotted a small opening between the piles of wood, he turned sideways and slipped through. Kate followed.

Behind the front row was a passageway lit only by sunlight slanting across the top of the wood. The walkway turned, doubling back between the second and third rows of wood. There the light was even dimmer.

"It's like a tunnel!" Kate exclaimed.

Anders put out his hands and groped ahead. Kate followed close behind. The walkway turned again between the third and fourth rows of wood. The farther they went, the darker it grew. Soon they needed to shuffle their feet to find their way.

"Anders?" Kate asked. She stopped.

The high piles of wood made her uneasy. If not stacked properly, they could fall in on her.

Anders halted for a moment, then crept on toward the back of the shed.

Unwilling to stay alone, Kate followed. When they lost all light, she grabbed hold of her brother's jacket.

A minute later Anders stopped again. Kate bumped into him. As they stood there, she heard something in the woodpile.

When Anders tried to go on, Kate tugged hard on his jacket. "What's the matter?" he asked.

"There's something here." Kate's voice was low. "Waiting in the darkness."

Anders snorted. "What a scaredy-cat!"

"I mean it. Listen."

As they waited quietly, she heard another quick movement. "There! That's what I heard before."

"Sure, Kate, and I know what it is."

"You do?" Kate listened. In the darkness the scurrying seemed closer.

"Yup. Just stand here without moving. You'll find out."

He loosened her fingers from his jacket. As Kate let go, he walked ahead without her.

"What're you doing?" Kate asked as he moved away.

In the darkness her brother's laugh sounded eerie. "Looking for the end of the tunnel."

"Anders!"

"Just stay there. I'll come back. Don't move, and you'll find out what's in the wood."

Kate bit her lip. With all her heart she wanted to stay with Anders. Yet she dreaded walking deeper into the blackness. Besides, she was curious. What had made that funny little noise?

In the next instant, something small and light ran across Kate's foot. From deep within, a scream rose in her throat.

Kate clapped her hand over her mouth. She was certain of one thing. There were mice in this woodpile!

Fighting against panic, she whirled around. Using her hands to feel her way, she stumbled back through the maze of logs. At last she reached the doorway.

"Kate!" Anders called. "Where did you go?"

"I'm out here!" she shouted, trying to sound unafraid. Quickly she pushed back her hair, straightened her coat, brushed the chips of wood off her clothing.

"Look what I found!" Anders exclaimed as he came out into the light.

In his hand he held a rolled-up blanket held together with a leather belt. When he unbuckled the belt, the blanket fell open. A plaid flannel shirt and two pairs of wool socks dropped to the ground.

"Strange!" Kate exclaimed. "Where did you find it?"

"At the very end of the tunnel. It made another turn and stopped along the back wall."

"Well, the shirt looks like it belongs to a man." Kate looked again at the high pile of wood. "How did he make the tunnel?"

"He took out whatever he needed to build a walkway. Stacked it up in front."

"That's hard work, moving all that wood. You're sure it's not boys from school?"

"Could be." Anders offered his lopsided grin. "But I think I'd have known about it. Usually I'm in on something like that."

Kate laughed. "You mean, you're *always* in on it!" She felt sure he was right. If it were just a prank, Anders would have known.

"Do you think someone's trying to live here?" Kate was curious again. As long as she didn't have to go back in the shed, she'd be all right.

Anders shrugged. "Nights are still mighty cold for sleeping out." He held up the shirt by the shoulders. "We've got one clue. It's probably a man, but not a very big one."

Kate stood back, studying the shirt. "You know, Anders, I keep thinking about that man in the mill. He was small enough to wear that shirt. Do you suppose—"

"Nope! That man was eleven miles away. Why would he be way out here?"

"There's something else," Kate said slowly. "To hide in a woodpile—to sleep outside when the nights still drop below freezing—"

She stopped, not wanting to say what she thought.

But Anders said it for her. "Whoever he is, he has to be desperate."

5

Back to School

$\mathcal{T}$hat night the weather turned even colder. Toward morning it snowed. When Kate saw the white blanket covering the earth, she remembered the bedroll and shirt in the woodshed. Anders had put them back in the place where he found them. What if someone really was trying to stay there?

Just thinking about the below freezing temperature, Kate felt chilled all through. She asked Anders about it. "If someone's trying to live in the woodshed—"

"Yup! He's freezing. But he's crawled back in, using the warmest spot."

Kate shivered. "He wouldn't stay there unless he's got something to hide." She didn't like that idea one bit.

After church and Sunday dinner, Kate found Anders taking Wildfire out of the barn. The mare's white star and four white socks shone in the cold sunlight. As Anders slipped the bridle over her head, she danced up and down, as though longing to be off.

"Where you going?" Kate asked, although she thought she knew.

"Over to school."

"Let me go too," Kate said.

When Anders mounted the mare, he reached down a hand and helped Kate up behind him. Wildfire pranced across the yard and down the hill on the shortcut through the woods. The trail led past Rice Lake, then wound between the trees to school.

Anders had brought along a candle and matches. While Kate waited outside, he walked back into the shed.

He came out shaking his head. "The clothes aren't there."

"So the man is gone."

"I think so."

Kate sighed, torn between relief and disappointment. She didn't like the idea of having someone desperate enough to stay in the woodshed. Yet her curiosity remained unsatisfied. Would they ever know who had hidden there?

On Monday morning Kate woke up feeling excited. After the long winter recess, she was glad to be going back to school. She looked forward to seeing Erik and her friend Josie every day.

After breakfast, Kate and Lars, Anders and Ben set out walking. With his six-foot three-inch height, Mama's brother stretched above six-foot Anders. By comparison, Kate felt her shortness even more.

Soft wet snow still clung to the trees. Long brown weeds, reaching above the white ground, sparkled with frost.

At a fork in the trail they met Erik and his younger sister, Chrissy. When Anders dropped back, Kate knew he was telling Erik about the woodshed. As the two boys caught up again, the teasing began.

"Wait till you see Miss Sundquist," Anders told Ben. "Prettiest teacher you'll ever meet."

"Yah?" Ben asked.

"And the *nicest* teacher you'll ever know," Kate said loyally. More than once, Miss Sundquist had been kind to her, helping Kate out of a difficult spot. "She's smart too. And a good teacher."

"Just your age, don't forget." Anders looked up at Ben. "She's eighteen."

"And the same age as my brother, John," Erik answered quickly.

Kate glanced at him. Was Erik warning Ben off? Did John like Miss Sundquist?

"Aw, c'mon, Erik," Anders said. "John's had over a year to speak his intentions."

"Speak his intentions?" Ben asked. "What do you mean?"

"Ask Miss Sundquist to marry him."

A red flush crept into Erik's neck, but Ben stopped in his tracks.

"Yah?" he asked again. "So, what does that matter to me? I'm just going to school to learn."

Before long, the trail brought them to the edge of a steep ridge. With the trees still leafless from winter, Anders and the others had a clear view of the one-room school. Below them, it nestled in a hollow, with smoke from the woodstove curling upward.

At the bottom of the hill, a creek flowed between them and the school building. Swollen by rain and melting snow, the water ran high and out of its banks.

Anders led all of them down the hill and across the large log that spanned the creek. Lars and Ben, Erik and Chrissy followed, as if without a thought.

By now Kate was used to crossing on the log, but she couldn't help remembering how she felt her first day of school. With every step she looked down at the cold water that rushed so close beneath her feet.

When they reached the schoolhouse, Miss Sundquist stood in the small entryway. The teacher was short—only a few inches taller than Kate. Miss Sundquist had blue eyes and light brown hair. Her lips widened in a smile of welcome.

Behind Kate came Anders, then Ben. As Miss Sundquist tipped back her head to look up at the tall Swede, she seemed to gulp.

"Miss Sundquist, this is Ben," Anders said politely. "Bernhard Lindholm from Dalarna, Sweden."

"He's Mama's brother," added Kate.

"Good morning, Bernhard," Miss Sundquist answered. Ben towered above her by at least a foot. "We're glad to have you

with us." The teacher smiled, but it was one of the few times
Kate had seen her look uneasy.

"*God dag*," Ben answered, sounding like *good dog*. But Kate
knew he was saying the Swedish words for hello.

"Do you know English?" the teacher asked. She seemed very
small standing next to Ben. "We speak only English in school
and on the playground."

"Yah," answered Ben. "I speak English. I want to learn to
read and write it."

Miss Sundquist nodded, and her usual teacher look settled
over her face. "Then you came to the right place. We'll have you
reading and writing in no time."

As soon as Ben took off his coat, Miss Sundquist led him into
the classroom. There she pointed to the largest desk the school
had to offer.

Ben tried to sit down. He twisted and turned, but couldn't
get his long legs underneath the desk.

Around him, the children snickered, then broke into laughter. Miss Sundquist looked at them, and they fell quiet.

Miss Sundquist's gaze searched the room. Then she turned
to Anders and Ben. "Take that table along the wall and that
bench. Put them here for a desk for Bernhard."

When the boys brought the table, they set it down behind
the two seats Anders and Erik always claimed. One thing was
certain. There'd be trouble ahead. Kate felt sorry for Miss Sundquist.

A moment later, the outside door opened with another rush
of cold air. From the entryway came a tinkly laugh, like a spoon
against a glass. Though Kate couldn't see the door, she knew
who it was.

Quickly Kate claimed a seat. Just as quickly she pulled off her
sweater and laid it on the desk across the aisle.

If the teacher let them stay in the seats they chose, Kate's best
friend would be right next to her. Josie would also be sitting
directly in front of Anders. As Kate twisted around, she saw her
brother's grin and knew he was pleased.

Soon Maybelle Pendleton swept into the classroom like a

queen before her subjects. Slender and of medium height, her eyelashes were dark and her eyes a deep brown. Most startling of all was the reddish brown hair that was the envy of all the girls. Today Maybelle wore her hair in *curls*!

Kate glanced around. Every other girl in school wore two pigtails. Kate alone had only one—a long black braid that hung down the center of her back. Now that braid seemed very ordinary next to Maybelle's curls.

"Anders, you must introduce me to your friend." Maybelle's voice sounded honey sweet.

"Not my friend, Kate's uncle," Anders said quickly. He paused, looking embarrassed. "I mean, he's my friend too. This is Ben, Maybelle. Ben Lindblom."

Maybelle bestowed her warmest smile, and Ben grinned.

Beyond Maybelle, Kate caught a glimpse of her best friend, Josie. Behind Maybelle's back, Josie made a sickly sweet face. She dropped into the seat Kate had saved, then twisted around to talk to Anders.

Kate also turned around. Erik, with his wavy brown hair and teasing eyes, sat directly behind her.

"'Mornin', Kate," he said now, as though he hadn't seen her on the trail to school.

"'Mornin', Erik," Kate replied in the same tone of voice. She tried to think of a smart remark, as she usually did. But in that moment she remembered how nice Erik had been when Mama's baby was born.

Kate smiled. "Top o' the mornin' to ye."

Erik grinned at her Irish greeting. Just then Miss Sundquist asked for attention.

With her lovely thick hair swinging about her shoulders, Maybelle slid into the seat in front of Josie. As she glanced at Kate, Maybelle looked down her long beautiful nose.

"Welcome back to school," the teacher said. "I'd like to introduce a new boy."

A nervous look crossed her face, then was gone. "Excuse me. I want to introduce a new young man, Bernhard Lindblom."

As the children stared, Ben leaped to his feet. Solemnly he

turned to each part of the room and nodded his head.

"Counting Bernhard, we have fifty-eight students registered this term," Miss Sundquist went on. "I see that you've picked out the seats you'd like. You can stay there if you do a good job. If you start talking to your neighbors, I'll arrange where you sit."

The teacher looked back toward Anders and Erik, then said, "Please rise for the pledge of allegiance."

Kate slid out of her desk and stood with her hand over her heart. "I pledge allegiance to the flag of the United States of America," she said in unison with the others. "And to the Republic for which it stands. . . ."

Kate stole a look at Ben. He stood facing the flag without speaking. *What does it mean to him?* Kate wondered. *He's a citizen of another country.*

As they finished the pledge, Miss Sundquist and the children bowed their heads. Together they said the morning prayer. "Give me clean hands, clean words, and clean thoughts. Help me to stand for the hard right against the easy wrong."

The students dropped into their seats, and Miss Sundquist spoke again. "I have an important announcement for you. We're going to have a box social on Saturday night."

"Box social?" Ben asked in a low voice. "What is that?"

"Shhhh," Erik whispered. "I'll tell you later."

"I want you to invite all the grown-ups you know," Miss Sundquist said. "If we raise a big amount of money, we'll add it to what we already have. Maybe we can buy an organ."

An organ? In her wildest dreams Kate had never dared to hope the school would buy a reed organ. *If we get one, I can play for the singing.*

"I need volunteers," said Miss Sundquist, "students who will help me that night, setting up and cleaning afterward."

Kate raised her hand. *Anything to get an organ,* she thought.

Miss Sundquist nodded, but looked beyond Kate. "I also need some boys to help. Anders?"

He groaned.

"And Erik? How about you?"

When Erik nodded, Maybelle's hand shot up. "I can help too, if you like, Miss Sundquist."

This time it was Kate who groaned. Maybelle heard and glared at her. But Kate didn't care. She knew how much Maybelle liked Erik.

As soon as Miss Sundquist assigned work to the older grades, she started helping the younger children near the front.

Ben poked Erik. "What is box social?"

"The ladies fix up boxes and fill 'em with really good food," Erik whispered. "The men bid on the boxes."

"Bid on them?" Ben asked. "What is that?"

"They call out how much money they'll pay. If more than one man wants a box, they bid against each other. The price goes up. The man who buys the box eats with the lady who brought it."

"Every lady brings a box?" Ben asked.

"Yup. But it's a secret—who brings which box. If you buy a box brought by a woman with five children, you have to eat with all the children."

"Does teacher bring a box?"

Erik looked uncomfortable. "My brother John will want to eat with her," he said stiffly. "I thought you came here to learn."

"Yah, I did." Ben winked at Kate. "I learn fast."

As Miss Sundquist looked their way, the boys stopped talking. Kate bent her head over her arithmetic book. No matter how hard she tried, Erik and Anders always finished the problems before she did. Yet Kate usually stayed ahead of them in reading and writing.

Just then she heard a strange sound—a soft scratching noise. Before Kate could think what it was, Miss Sundquist started toward the back of the room.

Passing Kate, she stopped at Ben's table. When the teacher asked Ben how far he had gone in school, Kate acted as if she were reading, but continued to listen.

Ben tried to explain, and the teacher kept asking questions. Clearly there was something she didn't understand.

"In arithmetic?" she asked, sounding puzzled. Though she

knew Swedish, Miss Sundquist couldn't break the rule about speaking English in school.

In that moment Kate heard the scratching noise again. It sounded like something secret, as though someone was trying not to be heard.

Kate turned around. Erik sat with his head lifted. He was also listening.

Who was making the noise? Where did it come from?

6

Boys Against the Girls!

*W*hat is it?" Kate whispered to Erik.

"Katherine," Miss Sundquist said. "This isn't the time to talk."

Kate whirled back to her work.

"Thataway, Kate!" Anders said in a loud whisper.

Kate risked a quick peek and saw the teacher's stern look at Anders. Then Miss Sundquist left Ben and returned to her desk.

Moments later, the teacher called Chrissy, Erik's third-grade sister. When she also asked Ben to come forward, he slowly unfolded his long legs and walked to the front of the room.

Chrissy took her place at the blackboard. Her short pigtails stood out at the two sides of her round face. She looked scared, as if wondering whether she could do what the teacher asked. When she turned to the board, the top of her head came to the bottom of Ben's chest.

Anders snickered. "Bet Miss Sundquist thinks Ben has only done third-grade work."

Kate stiffened, not wanting to see her uncle shamed in front of all the children. Ben was good with numbers. It was one area where he didn't have a language problem.

With his face to the blackboard, Ben looked sideways at Chrissy. When she picked up a piece of chalk, he picked up another piece.

Several children at the front of the room put down their books and waited to see what would happen.

When Miss Sundquist gave the first problem, Chrissy started writing immediately. Ben stood without moving, his head turned slightly, as though he were looking down and over. Was he trying to see what Chrissy wrote?

Gradually he followed Chrissy's lead, writing the numbers on the board, then the answer.

With the second problem, Ben again worked it just a bit behind the little girl.

Watching him, Kate felt uncomfortable. Was Ben waiting to see what Chrissy wrote, then copying her work?

Apparently the teacher wondered too, for the next time she gave Ben and Chrissy two different problems.

Oh, Ben! Kate thought. *You're going to get caught!*

Ben wrote down the problem, then hesitated, as if wondering what to do.

Just then Kate heard another strange noise. Or she thought she heard it. There was so much snickering, it was hard to tell.

"Has Ben done arithmetic before?" Josie whispered.

Kate nodded, but glanced around the room. All fifty-six heads were up, watching to see what would happen.

As Ben started working the addition, Kate breathed a sigh of relief. He even got it right!

With the next problem Ben wrote down the answer, then looked around. He seemed to know everyone was watching him.

The teacher gave him still more problems. Ben continued working, as though his life depended on having them correct.

Finally the teacher gave him three problems at one time. While she helped other children at their desks, Ben finished all his problems.

With a solemn face he turned toward the class. Next to him, Chrissy stood quietly, facing the children while waiting for Miss

Sundquist to check her work. Carefully Ben rested his elbow on the top of Chrissy's head.

When the snickers changed to giggles, Ben straightened. Holding his arm in front of his waist, he bent over in a low bow.

Across the room, students broke into laughter.

"That'll be all, Ben," Miss Sundquist said crisply. She looked around the class, warning the children not to laugh again.

"Yes, ma'am," Ben answered softly. Something in his voice told Kate that Ben knew he'd won.

Miss Sundquist stared at him, the teacher look in her eyes. Though she stood straight as an arrow, her head came below Ben's shoulder.

As Ben stared back, soft color crept into Miss Sundquist's cheeks. She lifted her chin and turned away.

Kate ducked her head into her book to keep from laughing. One part of her didn't want to see Miss Sundquist embarrassed. Up till now, no one had managed to stare her down. Another side of Kate liked seeing Ben come out best.

When he returned to his seat, the other students went back to their work. Kate had time to think about the noises she'd heard. What was causing them? Did they have anything to do with the person in the woodshed?

Kate could only wonder. But she felt sure of one thing. The strange sounds didn't come from inside the room.

———

At noon Kate ate her lunch, then hurried to the cloakroom. Along two outside walls were shelves for lunch pails. On the other walls hooks held coats and sweaters.

Kate pulled on her coat and went outside. While standing on the porch, she caught a movement out of the corner of her eye. The next instant a snowball hit her shoulder, splatting into her face.

Kate whirled around. Anders was crouched on the ground, a pile of snowballs next to him. The day had grown warmer, offering perfect conditions for packing snow.

Quickly Kate stepped back inside. Only girls remained in the classroom. "C'mon, Josie!" she shouted. "The boys want a snow-ball fight!"

Josie gulped down the bite in her mouth and jumped up.

"Boys against the girls!" Kate called to the others. "Help us beat 'em!"

As the younger girls hurried to put away their lunch pails, Maybelle tossed her head. "Snowball fights are just for boys!"

Halfway to the cloakroom, the girls stopped and turned toward Maybelle.

"That's not true," Kate answered from across the room.

Maybelle's curls bounced around her shoulders. "Girls don't play that way. What are you—a bunch of tomboys?"

Kate's chin shot up. "Girls defend themselves!"

Maybelle lifted a carefully arched eyebrow. "My mother says tomboys grow up to no good end."

Kate pretended she didn't hear, but Maybelle went on. "My mother says that if you play like boys, they'll think you are one. You'll never get married."

Kate's cheeks burned, and she knew they must be red with anger. She felt sure everyone in the whole room was listening. Some of the younger girls believed Maybelle and walked back to their seats.

Kate stalked over to Erik's sister, Chrissy. "You can help us," she said, speaking softly. "You can make snowballs, and Josie and I will throw them."

Chrissy's eyes sparkled. Hurrying into the cloakroom, she set down her lunch pail and pulled on her coat. She and her closest friends followed Kate out the door.

Maybelle's singsong chant followed them. "Katherine is a tomboy! Katherine is a tomboy!"

On the front porch, Kate peeked around the corner of the schoolhouse. The boys had already made a large number of snowballs. If they saw the girls now, there would be no contest.

Ducking out of sight, Kate pointed to the other end of the porch. Tiptoeing across, the girls jumped to the ground on the back side of the building.

Kate looked around. There wasn't enough snow to roll huge

balls and build a fort. Something else had to be done. They needed a barricade, and quickly, before the boys found them.

As her gaze settled on the woodshed, Kate remembered the tunnels. "Follow me," she said quietly.

Kate hurried around behind the shed. Working as fast as she could, she made a big mound of snowballs. The other girls followed her example.

Then Kate picked up as many snowballs as she could carry. Tucking them in her arms, she crept around the shed to the opening in the wood. "Let's hide," she whispered and hoped their noise would scare the mice away.

One by one the girls slipped into the walkway. Enough wood had been used so that Kate could see over the front row. But the littlest girls were safely hidden, out of sight behind the wall of wood.

Kate piled her snowballs at her feet. The rest of the girls did the same. Then Kate and Josie and Chrissy crept out, picked up the rest of the snowballs and passed them back into the hiding place.

At last Kate felt satisfied with their store of ammunition. With Josie at her side, she stood waiting for the boys to discover them.

When Anders rounded the corner of the schoolhouse, Kate fired a snowball in his direction. With full force it hit his chest. As snow sprayed up in his face, Kate laughed. They were even!

Anders reached down, pounded snow together, and hurled it at her. Kate ducked behind the stacked wood just in time. The snowball smashed into pieces against the hard surface.

Anders shouted to the boys. "C'mon! They're out here!"

The boys tumbled around the school, each with ammunition in hand. As a volley of snowballs headed their way, Kate and Josie ducked. Before the boys could make more, the girls stood up, firing rapidly.

Still hidden, the little girls passed their snowballs behind the wall. Grabbing the balls, Kate and Josie threw them, then ducked. The wall of wood kept them safe.

Time after time, the boys made new snowballs. Finally they started running out of snow and had to move farther out.

Kate called gleefully, "We beat you! Yaaaaay for the girls!"

The little girls set up a chant. "Girls beat the bo-o-oys! Ha, ha, ha, ha-ha!"

As the warning bell rang, signaling the return to class, Kate let out a whoop. They'd hit every single boy at least once!

After the boys retreated into the school, Kate let her little girls out. Quickly they ran to the porch. When they reached safety, Kate hurried to the girls' outhouse. Inside, she twirled the small piece of wood that locked the door.

Moments later, she heard snickers from close by, followed by silence. Were the boys planning another attack?

Soon Kate found out. One snowball after another hit the door with a loud thud. Then a snowball dropped through the opening above the door.

Kate stepped sideways, avoiding a direct hit. But the next snowball landed at the base of her head and slid down her back. Kate yelped with the cold.

From outside two boys laughed. Anders and Erik!

Crouching as far from the opening as possible, Kate waited. Two more snowballs dropped through, but neither one hit her.

Still Kate listened. Everything was quiet. Had the boys gone inside?

For a minute longer, Kate waited. If she didn't return to class, she'd be counted tardy and have to stay after school. How could she tell if the boys had left?

Looking around the inside of the outhouse, Kate searched for knotholes in the wood. When she found one, she put her eye against the wall and looked out. Suddenly a snowball hit the wood, half an inch from her eye.

Kate jumped back. Again, she waited. Again, no sound told her that the boys were still there. The final bell began to ring, signaling students to take their seats. If Kate ran, maybe she could still make it.

She unlocked the door and stormed out. A soft snowball splatted into her face.

Kate tried to wipe her eyes. "Stop it!" she yelled. Before she could turn, another snowball struck her wrist and dropped down her coat sleeve.

Whirling, Kate retreated into the outhouse. Pulling the door shut, she locked it again. Several more snowballs slammed against the wood.

"Dumb boys!" Kate muttered.

The bell stopped ringing, and Kate knew she was late. She tore open the door and hurried into school.

When she hung up her coat, the cloakroom was empty. Kate waited until Miss Sundquist was busy, then slipped into her seat.

A minute later the teacher noticed Kate. "Anders, Erik, and Katherine! You are to stay after school."

Kate sighed. It was bad enough having to stay after. If Papa found out, there would be even more trouble when they got home. They'd be punished again for misbehaving at school.

7

More Trouble

*D*uring the afternoon, Kate heard the strange noise once more. Unwilling to turn around and talk to Erik, she kept thinking about the sound.

What was it? A small animal that had worked its way in during winter? Whatever was making the noise, it came from different places.

Kate remembered the mice in the woodpile. Could they be also living in the school?

Yet that didn't seem quite right. Sometimes mice got between the walls at home. When they ran across a ceiling, it sounded like small scampering feet. Here she had heard sounds like that, but there were other noises, too—something different.

After school, Miss Sundquist asked Kate to straighten the cloakrooms and bookshelves and clean the blackboard. She asked Erik and Anders to sweep and wash the schoolroom floor. While Erik shoved the desks to one side, Anders carried water from the pump.

Each time the boys glanced her way, Kate looked off in a different direction. They'd started the fight. This was all their fault. If she had her way about it, she'd never speak to either of them again!

While dusting books, Kate had an idea. Before she could lose her nerve, she walked over to the teacher's desk.

"Miss Sundquist?" Kate spoke softly, keeping her back to the boys so they couldn't hear.

"Yes, Katherine?"

Kate cleared her throat. "Would you like some music for the box social? Anders and Erik and I could play together. Mr. Peters has been helping us."

"Mr. Peters?"

Kate knew the man's musical ability was respected through-out the area. "He's teaching Erik on the guitar and Anders on the fiddle. I play a traveling organ—a little pump organ that folds up like a suitcase."

"And the three of you could play some songs for us?"

"Yes, ma'am," Kate answered quickly. "At least two." But the minute she spoke, she felt scared. Could they really? They'd been practicing only a short time.

"That sounds wonderful!" Miss Sundquist said warmly. "Anders! Erik! I'd like to have the three of you play on Saturday night."

At the back of the room, Anders choked. Erik looked as if he couldn't believe what he'd heard. Kate smiled sweetly at them.

"Thank you, Kate, for telling me," Miss Sundquist said. "We'll look forward to your music."

"So will I," Anders growled.

When Kate walked past him, he muttered, "How could you do that to us? We aren't ready to play!"

"We'll never be more ready than now!" Kate answered. It would be their first opportunity to perform as a group. They could play well, she felt sure of it. Maybe it would be the beginning of her career as an organist!

By the time Anders and Erik finished washing the floor, the sun had slipped behind the steep hill back of the school. Miss Sundquist looked out the window.

"You may leave now," she said. "But I expect all of you to write a three-page paper about the example you want to give younger children during lunch hour. Turn it in by the end of the week."

Anders hurried out of the classroom. Kate and Erik went for their coats. The teacher had given them enough time to see their way home, but they couldn't fool around. Soon the dusk would change to darkness.

As Erik left the boy's cloakroom, he grinned at Kate. "Well, that wasn't too bad a punishment."

Kate wasn't ready to talk to him yet. She turned her back and stalked toward the entryway.

"You can hear me. Stop pretending."

Kate marched on. "I'm not pretending," she said to the door. "I don't want to speak to you."

Erik laughed. "You'll have to sometime."

Kate flipped her braid over her shoulder. "Not if I don't want to."

But Erik spoke softly. "Wondering about the noise?"

Kate jerked around, facing him. "What do you think it is?"

"Let's look outside. Anders heard it too."

As Kate and Erik jumped off the porch, they discovered Anders on the backside of the school. In spite of the wet ground, he lay on his stomach, trying to reach under the log building.

While supposedly carrying water, Anders had looked around. The men who built the school had brought in field stones and turned the flattest sides up for a foundation. On this side of the building, the stones were higher than on the front side. Anders had found a wide gap between two large stones.

"There's something in there," he said.

With his head against the bottom log, he strained to reach beneath the school. His broad shoulders kept him from whatever it was.

Finally he wiggled back and jumped to his feet. His jacket and overalls were wet and muddy from lying on the ground.

"Why don't you give it a try, Kate?"

"Me?" Kate backed away. "Not on your life! You're just trying to trick me again."

Anders raised his right hand. "There's really something there."

"Something like a thick, furry animal. Or mice running around!" Kate paused, wondering what Anders could manage to think up. "Or a snake!"

"Nope!" This time it was Erik trying to encourage her. "Not a snake! Not when it's still this cold."

Kate didn't think she could trust either of them. "If there's something under there, *you* get it!"

"I promise you, Kate." In the dying light her brother's eyes looked serious. "There's something there, but I think it's a tin can. Erik and I are too big to crawl close enough."

"Tell you what," Erik said. "Just to show you it isn't a trick, we'll put Anders' coat on the ground. You won't even have to get wet."

Kate looked from one to the other. Both of them seemed to be telling the truth. What if they were being honest, and she just walked away? She'd never know what was there.

"All right," she said, her curiosity getting the best of her. "But if you're teasing me, I'll never trust you again."

As soon as Anders spread out his coat, Kate lay down on her stomach and wiggled forward. She was small enough to creep between the stones. Half in and half out, she reached ahead, trying to feel the tin can.

"Say, Kate, maybe we're wrong," Anders called to her. "Snakes might be out this early."

In that instant Kate's hand touched down on something long and thin. As it moved, Kate scrambled backward. Her head bumped on the bottom log.

"Owwww!" she cried. Frantic to get out, she put down her hand again.

Suddenly she relaxed. She was only touching a long stick.

Again she reached forward. When she felt the edge of a can, she grasped it firmly. Carefully she backed out of the hole, pulling first the can, then the stick.

The tin can was partly filled with dirt. Kate felt disappointed. What a waste of time! And now she was wet from where her brother's coat didn't cover the ground.

Anders took the can and tipped it. Dirt fell out.

"Worms!" exclaimed Erik. Bending down, he picked up the stick Kate had found. Long and narrow, it had a piece of string tied to one end. At the end of the string was a bent safety pin.

In the growing dusk Erik looked thoughtful. "Whoever made the pole used whatever he could find."

"Isn't it early for fishing?" Kate asked. Across the road and beyond an area of bushes and reeds lay the lake for which the school was named. Ice still remained in the center.

"Early?" Erik shook his head. "Not with the warm weather we had before the snow."

Then Kate remembered. Near the shore, the ice had melted into cold dark water. Someone could stand there and fish.

"This line has been used lately," Anders said. "The worms are fresh—dug since the ground thawed."

He looked around, as though searching for more signs of the person who had been there. Dusk was quickly changing to darkness.

"Do you think that's what we heard?" Kate asked. "Someone hiding the pole while we were in school?"

The boys looked at each other. "Could be part of it," Erik said slowly.

"But not all of it." Kate knew that expression in his eyes. Erik wasn't satisfied. He wanted to know more.

Anders grinned. "Well, Kate, you better put the stuff back. Let's try to catch the person who put it there."

It wasn't until Kate was part way home that she realized how dirty she was from crawling under the school.

———

When Erik left them at the fork in the trail, Kate remembered that she was still supposed to be angry with her brother. She stalked off on the path without speaking.

"Truce," Anders said, talking to her back.

"Truce? Peace between us?" Kate laughed scornfully. "You and Erik were *mean*!"

"Not really. Snowballs are just part of winter."

"Well, it's spring."

"And our last chance to throw snowballs," Anders said.

"Sure, but look at all the trouble you caused—making me late, having to stay after. What's Papa going to say when we get home?"

"I'm sorry, Kate," Anders said, as humbly as Kate had ever heard him sound.

But she knew better. "What do you want?" she asked.

"Nothing." Anders sounded as innocent as a baby.

Kate halted in the middle of the path. "Oh, Anders, stop it. You know there's something you want me to do. You'd never apologize otherwise."

"Well, now that you mention it."

"See?" Kate asked. "I told you so!" She started walking again.

Anders kept up with her. "You know those three pages Miss Sundquist wants us to write?"

"I suppose you want me to write yours."

"I was just thinking how easy it would be for you. Why, you'd be able to write them in two minutes flat."

"Not two minutes," Kate answered. "Two hours." Her mind leaped ahead. What could she trade?

"One hour at the most," Anders said.

"Two, maybe even three."

"It's not three, and you know it."

Kate shrugged. "Well, do it yourself."

"Ahh, Kate, I don't want to spend all week writing some old pages."

"Neither do I." Kate quickened her steps. "I'll finish mine tonight and be done with it."

Anders walked just as fast. "That's what I mean. Do yours tonight, and mine tomorrow night."

"You're lazy. Besides, we're supposed to write about being *good* examples. You could do that in one sentence!"

"Ahh, c'mon, Kate."

Kate stopped again. In the darkness she faced him. "What'll

you trade? I'll help you, but you have to write it. Now, what'll you trade?"

"Trade?" Anders looked hurt, but Kate knew he was pretending. "My dear sister, I thought you'd do it out of the goodness of your heart. Think of all the times I've helped you."

Kate hurried on. "I'm thinking. I'm thinking I'd like to ride Wildfire some more." The spirited black mare with four white socks belonged to Anders.

"Once."

"Five times."

"Twice."

"Four times."

They reached an agreement at three times.

"And I mean three really long rides—for my valuable hints," Kate said.

"It's a deal!" Anders made a face, as though he'd gotten the raw end of the bargain. Yet as he opened the door to the kitchen, the corners of his mouth twitched up in a grin.

———————

Papa had gone to Trade Lake and had not yet returned. Mama was so busy with the new baby that she hadn't noticed how late Kate and Anders were. Neither Lars nor Ben had given them away. Kate felt relieved.

The next morning at school Josie leaned across the aisle. "Kate," she whispered.

"What's wrong?" Kate asked. When Josie looked like that there was usually a mystery to solve.

"Yesterday I didn't eat all my lunch."

Kate thought back to the day before. A lot of the girls had left part of their lunch in order to join the snowball fight.

"When I went home, I forgot my lunch pail in the cloakroom," Josie said. "I thought I'd eat the sandwich today. When I got here this morning, the pail was still here. But guess what?"

"What?"

Josie's eyes widened. "The sandwich was gone."

"Gone?"

"Every single crumb!"

"Strange," Kate said. "Maybe one of the boys ate it."

Josie shook her head. "They have their own cloakroom. Usually they don't go into ours. Besides, I've left sandwiches before. Up till now, no one's taken a nibble."

When Miss Sundquist asked for attention, Kate forgot about what Josie said. That is, she forgot until later that morning.

To check what they had learned, Miss Sundquist called the oldest students forward. As Kate walked toward the benches at the front of the room, she glanced up. Above the blackboard were pictures of George Washington and Abraham Lincoln. For many years they had looked down on the students who came and went.

If you were alive, you'd know lots of secrets, Kate thought. With hands on either side to brace herself, she sat down on her usual bench. It was no longer wobbly!

To test it out, Kate tried to rock. In all the time that she'd attended the school, the bench had wiggled beneath her weight. Only yesterday she'd been afraid it would fall apart. Now the bench felt solid and strong.

She glanced up to find Erik watching her. "Did you fix it?" she asked.

Erik sat on another bench, his long legs stretched out in front of him. He shook his head.

Kate turned toward Anders. "Did you?"

"Aw, Kate, you know me better than that!"

Kate grinned. "Right! I never should have asked." But she tucked the fixing of the bench away at the back of her mind. *What's going on around here?* If not Erik, who would repair it?

Then Kate remembered Josie's sandwich. The footprints in the Hickerson Mill. Little things, all of them. Yet Kate had learned to watch for little things. Especially when something mysterious might be happening.

8

Unhappy Surprise

$\mathcal{T}$he rest of the morning Kate listened for any odd noise. Not once did she hear anything strange. Just the same, during lunch hour she walked around the outside of the school. She couldn't get over the feeling that they were missing some clue.

On the east side of the school a baseball diamond filled the area between the building and the road. On the south end was the porch, on the back or west side, the woodshed. Nothing seemed out of the ordinary.

By the time Kate reached the north end of the building, she was almost ready to give up. Then she looked up and discovered a small door, just beneath the peak of the roof. Built of the same siding as the upper part of the building, the door blended into the wall.

Aha! Kate thought. Filled with curiosity, she went back into the school. Quickly she searched the classroom and two cloakrooms, but discovered no opening in the ceiling.

When she found Anders and Erik, she told them about the door.

"There's no way to get up there," her brother said.

"All it takes is a ladder."

"Yup. And I know where the ladder is. Someone put it in the wrong place. It's along the back wall of the shed."

"You mean *inside* the shed?"

Anders nodded. "We'd have to move half the wood to get it out."

"No one could possibly use it?"

"I promise you, Kate. No one has used that ladder for a long time."

But Kate wasn't satisfied. Deep down, she still felt curious. Somehow she'd figure out a way to learn what was behind that door.

––––––––

After school, Kate, Anders, and Erik walked to Four Corners to meet with Mr. Peters, their music teacher. Together they practiced the songs they would play at the box social.

"If you come back Saturday morning, I'll help you again," Mr. Peters promised.

By the time Kate and the boys returned to Windy Hill Farm, it was too late to take Wildfire out. All the next day, Kate kept thinking about riding the beautiful black mare.

As soon as Miss Sundquist dismissed them, Kate hurried home. Over the winter Anders had often given her tips on how to handle a horse. Kate had gone beyond wondering what might go wrong to really enjoying a ride.

Today Anders helped her catch the mare and slip on the bridle. Reins in hand, Kate pulled herself onto Wildfire's bare back.

As usual, Anders took up his role as teacher. "She hasn't been out for a couple days. She's going to want to run."

Kate looked forward to that. During the winter she had learned how to nudge Wildfire into a canter.

"Have her warm up first," Anders said as he stroked the star on the mare's forehead. "Make sure you hold her in enough so you don't lose control."

Kate nodded, impatient to be off.

"She's got to know you're boss," Anders went on. "When you pull her in, tug evenly on both reins. If you tighten just one rein, you'll pull her head around too fast. She might lose her balance and fall down."

Again Kate nodded. As Anders stepped back, she lifted the reins and nudged the horse. Wildfire started toward the main road.

"Stay close in case you need help!" Anders shouted.

Kate turned and grinned. She wouldn't have trouble. With her spirit riding high, she lifted her free hand to wave. Then the corner of the barn shut out her view of Anders.

Kate breathed deep, welcoming the warm air and the sense of freedom a ride always gave her. At first she walked the mare and looked around.

The dirt trail rose and fell with the rolling hills. All of the late snow had disappeared. In the hollows cold, dark water reflected branches still bare of leaves.

Kate nudged Wildfire into a trot. Soon they rounded a sharp bend in the trail. Suddenly a partridge flew up, directly in front of the horse.

The mare jerked, but Kate held her steady. As Wildfire settled back down, Kate felt grateful for what she'd learned. Once the partridge would have sent her flying off the horse.

A bit farther on, the trail stretched out straight and long between the trees. Kate nudged the mare into a canter, and wondered how fast she could run. She'd never let the horse really go. This might be a good place to try.

For an instant longer Kate thought about it. Then she dug in her heels.

Wildfire leaped forward into a gallop. As her long black legs stretched out, the trees seemed to fly past. Up a slight slope she kept her speed. When the road leveled out, she increased her pace.

The mare's hooves pounded on the dirt. One moment Kate felt scared. The next she felt excited. She didn't want to slow down, yet the main road lay ahead.

Pull evenly, Anders seemed to say as Kate tightened the reins.

When Wildfire obeyed, Kate leaned forward to talk in her ear. "Good girl!" The mare had done what she asked!

On the way back, Kate nudged the horse into a canter, then a gallop once more. Again Wildfire moved ahead or slowed down with her commands. By the time Kate reached the farmyard, she felt as if she'd opened the biggest gift in the world.

Anders was waiting outside the barn. As Kate slid down from Wildfire's back, he took the reins. "Pretty good ride, huh?"

Kate's excitement spilled over into laughter. "Good ride! Good horse!" Helping her brother with his three pages would be worth it.

In the barn Anders led the mare into her stall. Kate took off Wildfire's bridle and rubbed her down.

When Kate finished, she went searching for Anders. Quickly she climbed a ladder to the hayloft and poked her head through the opening in the floor.

In the center of the loft a large mound of hay still remained from last year's bumper crop. Anders stood on the top of the mound, clinging to a long rope attached to the track in the ceiling.

As Kate watched, Anders leaped off, swung to one end of the barn, then back across the hay to the other end. When he crossed the hay a second time, he dropped, landing right in the center.

"Want a turn?" he called when he caught sight of Kate.

As she climbed into the mound, Anders tossed her the rope. Grasping it with both hands, Kate leaped into the air. Back and forth she swung in an arc, liking the feeling.

Then she looked down. Her stomach seemed to leave her.

How could the floor be so far away? If she dropped at the wrong place, she'd land on wood. Or even worse, fall through one of the holes for throwing down hay. Kate clenched her hands as though she'd never let go.

When the rope slowed down, Anders called to her. "Jump, Kate!"

Like it or not, she'd have to let go of the rope. There was only one place to land safely—in the deep pile of loose hay. What if she missed?

Kate waited until just above the hay. Then she opened her hands and dropped.

For a split second Kate felt breathless. The next instant soft hay surrounded her, cushioning her fall. Rolling over, she laughed. It struck her funny that she'd been so scared.

She'd fallen off center, away from the spot where Anders usually landed. As she stood up, Kate felt something beneath her foot. Kneeling down, she pushed aside the hay and uncovered an old battered suitcase.

Holding it up, Kate called, "Anders!"

"What've you got?" Climbing through the hay, he reached her. "A suitcase?"

"Kind of a strange place for one."

"You betcha. I helped with haying last summer, and we sure didn't leave a suitcase."

"It's awfully light," Kate said. Laying the dark brown suitcase on top of the hay, she opened the latches and lifted the cover.

"It's empty!" Anders was clearly disappointed.

So was Kate. "Why would someone hide an empty suitcase in a hayloft?"

Her brother looked as puzzled as she felt. "You found it right here?"

When Kate nodded, Anders looked around as though fixing the spot in his mind.

"See that mark on the side wall?" Anders pointed. "And there's another one on the end wall. You wouldn't see them unless you looked. Whoever hid that suitcase put it where those two lines meet."

"To make sure he could find it again," Kate said slowly. "How long do you think it's been here?"

Anders shook his head. "No way to tell. Whoever hid it knew we wouldn't get to that hay for a while."

As Kate stared down at the empty suitcase, her mind leaped from one idea to the next. Just thinking about the whole thing made her knees feel weak.

"Anders? Do you think the man stayed here?"

"Could be. At least overnight."

"Why would he leave a suitcase?"

"Maybe it's easier to travel without it."

"To roll up whatever clothes he isn't wearing in a blanket?"

Anders nodded. "Yup. Tie it with a belt. Carry it over his shoulder."

"Like the man who used the woodshed."

"Yup." For once Anders didn't tease her. His seriousness made the whole thing seem even worse.

"If he left the suitcase where it could be found . . ." Kate's voice trailed off. The empty feeling was back at the pit of her stomach. "That means he's planning to come back."

9

Secret Signals

*A*nders nodded. "Yah sure, you betcha." A grin lit his eyes. "Some dark night, when you're milking the cows, he'll drop through a hole from the hayloft!"

"Oh, Anders!"

"Without making a sound he'll creep across the floor. On little cat feet, he'll sneak up behind you. When your back is turned, he'll pounce on you!"

Kate stood up. Not for anything would she let Anders know that she felt scared right down to her toes. She longed to stuff her fingers in her ears so she couldn't hear him.

Instead, she flipped her long braid over her shoulder. "I thought *I* was the one with imagination!"

Anders laughed. Even in those few minutes, shadows had started to creep across the hayloft. "Why don't you go find Papa?"

"Why don't *you*?"

"Because the man might still be here," Anders said calmly.

Without another word Kate scrambled out of the hay onto the floor. As she headed for the ladder, the corners of the loft seemed darker than ever before.

When Papa came, he and Anders walked across the hay, checking each part of the large mound to make sure no one remained in the loft.

"What's going on around here?" Papa said at last.

Kate had been wondering the same thing while Anders and Papa searched. "Do you think it's the man I saw in the mill?" she asked. "The Thomas in the newspaper?"

Papa stroked his beard, his eyes thoughtful. "I don't know."

"He could have come home with us."

"With *you*?"

"In the back of the wagon," Kate said. "Under the canvas. I saw it move once. I thought it was just the rough road—that we'd bounced into a hole."

Papa sighed. "Whoever the man is, I don't like it. I usually don't lock our doors, but I'll start tonight."

All through supper Kate felt upset. She couldn't get the hidden suitcase out of her mind. Nor could she stop wondering about the man who might have stolen a ride with them.

Later, while Kate and Ben and Anders studied at the kitchen table, she spoke up. "With all that's going on, we need a way to talk to Erik."

"I was just thinking the same thing," Anders said. "We haven't sent Lutfisk with a message for a while."

He scribbled a note. "Let's make sure Lutfisk doesn't forget what to do."

Opening the back door, Anders called. When the dog came bounding up, Anders knelt down to pet him, then fastened the note to his collar.

"Go get Erik," he commanded, pointing toward Lundgren's farm. The dog streaked off.

"We're training him to take messages back and forth," Kate explained to Ben.

"Yah, that is good," her uncle answered. "That's what Swedes do. Swedes use a goat or cow horn. Or a *lur*." The word sounded like *lure*. When Ben came to Windy Hill Farm, he had brought the long narrow horn with him.

Kate felt curious. "Ben, how did you call between farms?"

"We have signals." Ben stood up and got his lur from an out-of-the-way corner of the kitchen. Returning to the table, he said, "Girls use them when they take the cows and goats up in the mountains."

"For pasture?" Anders asked.

"Yah. Farmers don't have much grass near their buildings. They have to save what they have to make hay for winter. So girls or women take the animals away—ten, twelve miles, maybe more, for the summer."

"The girls stay up there?" Kate wanted to know.

"They live in small settlements. Each girl has a cabin, a small barn, and a milk house where she makes cheese." When Ben couldn't remember a word, he used Swedish, and Anders translated for Kate.

"In the morning each girl takes her animals to a pasture set aside for her," Ben said. "The girl sings to her cows and goats as she herds them. They know her voice."

"So every girl is alone all day?" Kate asked.

Ben grinned. "To fight the bear and wolf."

Kate swallowed hard. She wasn't sure if Ben was teasing or not. Already he knew how she felt about finding a bear in their woods.

"That's why a girls plays a cow horn or a goat horn," Ben said. "And sometimes, the lur."

"To send signals." Kate decided Ben was serious. From across the table she looked at Anders. This was exactly what they needed!

Ben nodded. "Tunes that are signals. Everyone knows what those tunes mean. 'My goat is lost.' Or, 'My cow is lost.' Or, 'Help! I am in trouble.' "

Kate felt excited. "Ben, could you teach Anders and me to play the lur?"

Her uncle grinned. "Yah. Like Miss Sundquist teaches me to read and write."

"Only one thing wrong," Anders said. "Erik doesn't have a way to answer back."

Ben shrugged. "That is easy. I will make one for him."

"You can *make* a lur?" Anders asked.

"Yah, I make good lurs. From earliest time—" He stopped. "When I was a small boy, I watch my father make them."

He patted the long, thin horn. "This one I made. I brought it with me because the tone is very good."

"And you can make one for Erik?" Kate asked. "Soon?"

Ben nodded. "If I work fast, the sound may not be so good."

"The important thing is that we can call each other," Kate answered.

Solemnly Ben nodded. "Tomorrow I will start. In time of trouble you can call back and forth."

Kate felt better just knowing that Ben understood. Yet as she thought more about it, she grew uneasy. Even Ben realized that something around here was very wrong.

————

When school let out the next afternoon, Kate and Anders and Ben hurried home. Erik came too. He wanted to learn how to make a lur.

At Windy Hill Farm, Ben took an axe and led them into the woods. There he searched for just the right spruce tree. When he found it, he cut it down, lopped off the branches, and carried the trunk to an empty stall in the barn. There he peeled the bark and started shaping the wood into the four-and-a-half-foot length that he needed.

As Ben worked, he hummed with satisfaction, as though glad to be doing something he liked. But Kate remembered his words. "In time of trouble you can call back and forth."

The next day, Erik came home with them again. They all trooped out to the barn to watch Ben work on the lur.

Beneath his skillful hands, the wood was becoming a long pipe—narrow at one end with a slight bell shape at the other.

When Ben finished smoothing the wood, he sawed the long

piece lengthwise, down through the center. Carefully he began hollowing out the two halves.

After a time Kate asked, "Will you play your lur from Sweden? Erik's never heard you."

When Kate brought the lur from the house, Erik looked it over. "It's like pictures of a horn from the Alps," he said. "But the shape is a little different. And it must be smaller."

Ben set down his tools. Taking the lur outside, he cupped one hand around the small end. With his other hand he supported the long pipe.

Lifting the lur to his lips, Ben blew high and low tones, as though warming up. The clear notes sounded much like a trumpet, but more mellow. Because there were no valves or finger holes in the horn, Ben produced the tones with the control of his breath and lips.

"It'll carry a long distance," Erik said when Ben stopped.

The tall Swede nodded. "Eight or ten miles, maybe more."

Erik looked pleased. "No trouble hearing it at our farm."

"In the old country only girls play the lur," Ben said. "But when I make one, I play songs."

He handed Kate the long horn. "You want to learn?"

A grin lit Anders' face. "Think you can manage to blow it, Kate?"

"Of course," she said stiffly. "Why not?"

"Well, come to think about it, maybe you'll do better than any of us. You have more wind."

Kate turned her back on her brother as Ben showed her how to hold the lur. "Now blow," he said.

Kate puffed out her cheeks, filling them with air.

"Keep your cheeks in!" Ben exclaimed.

Once again, Kate tried. But not a sound came from the horn. Anders snickered.

"Just wait," Kate said. "You won't do any better."

"Smile," Ben told her.

When Kate didn't understand what he meant, Ben pulled the edges of his lips to each side as if he were smiling. He blew a thin stream of air between his lips.

Kate managed to make a noise, but it sounded like one big *blaaaat*. Anders did no better. Then Erik picked up the horn.

Ben stopped him. "Like this." He put his fingers to his lips and pushed them together. "Then *buzzz*."

On the first try, Erik sounded the lur the way it was meant to be played.

"That is good!" Ben exclaimed.

With each try Erik seemed to improve. Some of his notes even sounded clear and long.

When Ben returned to his carving, Kate and the boys went to the granary to talk. Sitting down on the floor, they leaned back against large bins for storing grain.

"We need to work out signals," Kate said. "Ben has tunes, and each tune means something."

Erik shook his head. "If we play tunes, it'll take a long time before we're good enough. One missed note, and we'd mix up the signal."

Anders grinned. "We aren't off to a very good start."

Kate giggled, remembering how she and Anders sounded. "Do we need to tell who's calling? If someone else played the lur, it wouldn't be a real signal."

"We could begin that way," Erik said. "Like we're saying, 'This is Kate,' or 'This is Anders.' "

Kate had brought along a pencil and a piece of paper. She started writing.

"We should be able to say, 'Come here,' " Anders said. "And 'Danger.' If we played 'come' and 'danger' at the same time, it could mean, 'Come at once, but be careful.' "

To that Erik added, "Meet me at the fork in the trail," and, "Meet me at school."

Kate also added Wildfire's name. "Is that all?" she asked.

"We better keep it simple," Erik told her. "We don't want to get mixed up."

"But what will the signals be?" Kate asked.

"I know!" Erik answered. "We'll use the Morse code. I read about it in school the other day."

Anders stared at his friend. "That's a lot of work to learn."

"Not if we use just the signals we need. Remember the telegraph operator at the train station? He taps a little knob. The sound goes over the wire. If he presses it short, it's a dot. Longer, it's a dash. We could play high or low notes, in any pattern we want."

Kate grinned. "You mean any notes we're *able* to play!"

"Sure," Erik said. "People would listen to the tune, but that wouldn't matter. What *would* matter is the rhythm. A short toot for a dot. A longer toot for a dash."

Erik started. *"Daaaaa, da, da, daaaah!"*

Anders laughed. "You got it, old buddy. It's like the signal Kate and I used when she first came here. We rapped on wood."

"It would work," Kate said. "Even if we played really awful! We'll just listen to the rhythm!"

Erik nodded. "We'll get that book at school and work out the signals."

"So all we have to do is learn how to blow!" Anders liked that idea.

Kate scrambled up. "Let's go back and play Ben's lur some more. We have to at least make decent sounds."

———

Ben worked on the new lur every chance he got, hollowing out the two long pieces of wood. By Saturday afternoon the pipe looked so thin that Kate wondered how he managed to keep from breaking through the wooden sides.

"Thanks, Ben," Kate told him as she watched him work.

Ben grinned. *"Tack,* you mean." The word sounded like "tock," but was the Swedish word for thanks.

"Tack," Kate said. Ben liked to hear her speak Swedish. *"Tack* for all the work."

At the same time she was teaching him English. "Now you say *thanks!"*

Her uncle laughed. "Just you wait," he said. "When Miss Sundquist gets done with me, I will write and talk like an American!"

"Ben? Are you sweet on Miss Sundquist?"

"For shame, child!" Ben drew his face into a sour expression. "You should not ask such questions!"

But Kate caught the teasing in his eyes. "You are, aren't you?"

Ben grinned. "You find out the box she brings to the social. Then tell your wonderful uncle from Sweden."

———————

That evening Kate washed the supper dishes as quickly as she could. Then she carried a pitcher of warm water and a kerosene lamp up to her bedroom.

Quickly she changed into her good dress. The blue made her eyes seem even bluer. She'd borrowed Mama's curling iron and wanted to try it.

Unbraided, Kate's long hair fell down her back, looking thick and shiny. As she brushed it out, Kate studied herself in the mirror.

Her black hair waved softly around her face, but she didn't feel satisfied with the bangs above her forehead. She thought about Maybelle and her beautiful auburn hair. When Maybelle wore curls, her hair seemed to bounce around her shoulders. *I'd like curls as nice as hers*, Kate thought.

She turned up the flame of the lamp, then set the steel end of the curling iron inside the glass chimney. The two wooden handles rested on the glass and held the iron above the flame.

When the iron seemed hot enough, Kate grasped the wooden handles and slipped a strand of hair between the pinching ends. Turning the iron, she wrapped her hair around it. But when she loosened her bangs, they had no curl.

The next try Kate heated the iron longer. Again she twisted a strand of bangs around the end of the iron. As she held it close to her head, her scalp felt painfully hot.

It'll be worth it, she promised herself. *I can handle a little pain to be beautiful. Maybe Erik will think I'm pretty.*

In the next instant the smell of something burning filled the room.

Filled with panic, Kate loosened the iron. Pieces of hair fell to the floor!

10

Highest Bidder

*K*ate looked in the mirror, unable to believe what she was seeing. One portion of her bangs still had its usual soft wave. The rest was burned off, close to the hairline.

Just then Anders called up the stairs. "Kate! We're going to be late! What's keeping you?"

Kate grabbed her brush and tried to pull the remaining bangs over the burned-off part. But her good hair wouldn't lie right.

Catching up a glass, she filled it with water. As she tipped the glass over her bangs, the water splattered onto her dress.

Again Kate took up the brush. When it touched the tender skin just below her hairline, she yelped with pain.

Leaning forward, she peered into the mirror again. A blister was already forming on her forehead.

Kate groaned. Carefully she brushed her wet bangs across the burned-off part. At last the hair lay almost flat.

There was not even a minute for braiding the rest of her hair. Kate pulled it back with a ribbon and let her long hair hang down. She was almost ready when Anders called from beneath the floor grate into her room.

"Kaaaate! Mr. Peters will be waiting for us. He doesn't like to wait!"

"I'm coming, I'm coming!" Kate hurried down the stairs.

In the kitchen Anders raised his head and sniffed. "What's that awful smell?"

Kate pulled on her coat before Anders could ask more questions. *We've got all the way to school,* she thought as she hurried outdoors. *Maybe my hair will air out.*

She wrapped a long scarf around her head and pulled it farther forward than usual. As she and Anders started toward the path, a sliver of moon rose above the trees.

Erik was waiting at the fork in the trail. Kate followed the boys, nearly running to keep up with their long strides. The closer they came to school, the more she dreaded being there. All week long she'd looked forward to playing for the grown-ups. Now everything had changed.

When they reached the hill behind the school, Kate felt the hair above her forehead. Her bangs felt stiff and wet.

With dragging steps she followed the boys down the path into the schoolhouse. In the cloakroom she slowly hung up her coat. She wished she could stay there and hide.

This time it was Erik who called her. "Kate!"

He and Anders stood in the main room, just outside the girls' cloakroom. When Kate came out, Anders looked at her with a strange expression in his eyes. "What's the matter with your bangs?"

"I wet them down," Kate said quickly.

"Are you sure that's all?" asked Erik. "It looks like something's wrong."

Kate's heart started beating faster. "I'm sure," she said stiffly. Not for anything would she tell the boys what had happened.

Just then Maybelle swept through the door from outside. For the first time in her life, Kate felt glad to see her. *The boys will forget about my hair. They'll just look at Maybelle.* Right now that seemed a wonderful idea.

"Hello, Anders," Maybelle said, her voice dripping with honey.

Anders grinned, but Maybelle turned away from him.

"And Erik." Maybelle's brown eyes glowed in the lamplight.

Her smile made it seem years instead of hours since she'd last spoken to him.

Erik nodded, but looked away toward Kate. Maybelle lifted her dainty nose and sniffed.

A scared feeling rushed through Kate. *She can't possibly smell my hair.*

But Maybelle's gaze went straight to Kate's bangs. She smiled. "Katherine, whatever is the matter?"

The words sounded sweet, but Kate knew Maybelle wasn't being kind. "Why, nothing," Kate answered, trying to keep her voice steady.

"But, Katherine, there *is*." Maybelle's voice grew louder with each word. Nearby, a young farmer and his girl turned to look.

Maybelle moved closer. "You know, Katherine, it looks as if you have a real problem."

Kate stepped back from the taller girl. Somehow Maybelle always made her feel like a small child holding on to her mother's apron.

Maybelle's hand darted out, touching Kate's bangs. Grabbing the good strand, she pulled it aside. "Did you burn off your hair?"

Kate felt the warm flush of embarrassment leap into her face. It seemed that every person in the room had turned to look.

Worst of all, now Erik and Anders *knew*. They would never let her forget.

Anders stared at Kate's bangs and grinned. A laugh started, deep in his throat, and worked its way up, until it seemed to fill the entire school.

Fighting against tears, Kate turned away. As she fled to the cloakroom, she saw Erik bite his lip.

He wants to laugh too! Kate was used to her brother's teasing, but she cared what Erik thought.

In the little room, Kate buried her face in her coat. Sobs tore at her throat, and her shoulders shook.

Miss Sundquist found her there. "I want to help you," she said.

Kate heard the kindness in the teacher's voice and sobbed harder. Finally she lifted her head long enough to ask, "How can

I possibly play the organ? I look *awful!*" Her words ended on a wail.

Quietly Miss Sundquist began talking. "You know, I did the same thing once. It was a curling iron, wasn't it?"

Kate nodded, but kept her face buried in her coat.

"I let it get too hot, and it took a clump right out of the side of my head."

Kate turned and looked into Miss Sundquist's eyes. "You did?"

"I did," Miss Sundquist said, her voice solemn.

Suddenly Kate giggled. Miss Sundquist laughed, too, and it sounded almost like Kate's giggle. For a moment they were friends instead of teacher and student.

Miss Sundquist's smile was soft and warm. "It'll seem forever, but your bangs will grow out. I promise you."

As Kate's trembling stopped, she rubbed her wet cheeks.

"Let me help you." The teacher disappeared, but in a minute was back with a towel dipped in cold water. "Wipe under your eyes."

When Kate finished, the teacher handed her a powder puff and led her to the mirror. "Just pat away the redness." She helped Kate comb her hair back over the burned-off spot.

Kate drew a long, deep breath. She dreaded returning to the other room. Yet she couldn't let Miss Sundquist down.

Tonight the teacher's light brown hair was drawn up in soft curls on top of her head. In the light of the lantern her blue eyes sparkled. Always Kate thought she was pretty, but never more so than now.

"Do you need to blow your nose again?" Miss Sundquist asked. She reached into the pocket of her coat.

As she pulled out a handkerchief, a bright yellow ribbon fell to the floor. Quickly the teacher picked it up and stuffed it back into her pocket.

But Kate had seen the ribbon. As though nothing had happened, she took the handkerchief. She blew her nose, feeling almost happy inside. Ben had asked her to find out which box belonged to the teacher. Kate had almost forgotten. Now she felt sure that she would recognize the right box.

By the time Kate walked into the classroom, Anders stood at the front, warming up on his fiddle. Erik sat nearby, his head tipped to listen as he tuned his guitar. Mr. Peters had opened the traveling organ and was looking around for Kate.

Maybelle stood at one side of the room, like a cat ready to pounce. Staying as far from Maybelle as possible, Kate started forward.

Josie stopped her. "Erik told me," she said as she gave Kate a quick hug. "I'm sorry."

Beyond Josie, Kate saw Erik watching. He smiled, but didn't seem to be laughing at her. Just the same, Kate tossed her head and looked away.

"All set, Kate?" asked Mr. Peters. "Miss Sundquist wants to start soon."

As Kate sat down at the small organ, her hands trembled. She was too late for the warm-up she badly needed. Placing her fingers on the keys, she played a few runs and missed several notes.

When she looked up, Anders was watching, a worried frown on his face. Kate glared at him.

Mr. Peters sat down on a nearby bench, as though ready to help if they needed it. Kate's thoughts tumbled in a thousand directions. *How can I possibly play when I feel so awful?*

For over a year, Kate had wanted to play the organ for others. Often she had longed to play the way Jenny Lind sang. Always the Swedish nightingale had made people feel better because they enjoyed her music. But now? Kate wished she could sneak outside, into the darkness. *Everyone will see my hair and laugh!*

Then she remembered that long-ago day when she'd been afraid to play the organ in front of Erik. "Think of one person who encourages you," Mr. Peters had said.

As the grown-ups slipped into the desks, Kate thought about his words. One person—who could it be?

Certainly, Mama encouraged her to play, and Papa as well. Mama was home with the baby, but Papa had promised to be here. Where was he?

Kate searched the big seats toward the back of the room. He wasn't there. Instead, Kate found Papa leaning against the wall.

Their gaze met, and Papa grinned.

Kate smiled back. In that moment she felt better. *I'll play for him*.

When Miss Sundquist asked for everyone's attention, the room grew quiet. "We are privileged to have a new music group with us tonight," she said, then introduced Kate, Anders, and Erik. "Please welcome these musicians with a warm round of applause."

As the clapping rose around them, Kate felt overwhelmed by fear. Anders and Erik looked her way, and she froze, unable to give the signal to begin.

The boys waited, with the stillness seeming to stretch out forever. Kate stared at the music for the "Battle Hymn of the Republic."

Then, softly, from nearby, Kate heard Mr. Peters count. "One, and two, and three, and—"

Somehow they all started together. "Mine eyes have seen the glory of the coming of the Lord—" Kate's thoughts ran along with the notes.

But her hands shook. She missed one note, then another. In her nervousness she forgot to pump her feet to let air into the organ. Suddenly it moaned.

Kate gulped and pumped furiously. "His truth is marching on!"

She tried to think about Papa wanting to hear her play. Her hands steadied.

"Glory! glory, hallelujah! Glory! glory, hallelujah!"

By the end of the chorus, Kate's notes sounded sure and strong, blending with the guitar and fiddle. The second verse went even better.

As soon as the audience stopped applauding, Kate started the second song, "I Dream of Jeanie With the Light Brown Hair." This time she and the boys played without missing a note.

Applause surrounded them, loud and long. When the three finished taking their bows, Mr. Peters said, "Well done!"

Kate felt grateful. Mr. Peters always meant what he said. Just the same, she glanced toward the back of the room. Papa smiled and lifted one arm, as if in victory.

In that moment not even Kate's burned hair mattered as much. Papa liked what they had done! It was his praise she cared about most.

Then Miss Sundquist stepped forward. The room quieted. "We're ready to begin auctioning the boxes," she said. "Remember, all of the money goes to the organ fund."

August Cassel, the auctioneer, held up a box. "Here's a beauty," he said. "What am I offered? All for a good cause, folks!"

The bidding started slow, then picked up. Each woman there, whether married or single, had brought a box filled with food, decorated in the most attractive way possible.

As the men called out their bids, Kate looked over the box being sold. Set between large red and white hearts were bright red ribbons. No yellow ones.

But where was Ben? And how could Kate let him know if she did decide which box belonged to the teacher?

Soon an older man claimed the box, and Mr. Cassel held up another. Kate's gaze swung around the room. Ben wasn't there. With his great height she'd have seen him, Kate felt sure.

Before long, the auctioneer held up a box decorated with paper roses.

"Ohhhhh!" sighed a woman near Kate. An excited buzz of approval filled the room.

"Well, gents, let's hear your bids for the prettiest box you'll ever see! Just imagine all the good food inside!"

Kate stared at the box. Here and there, among the paper roses, were white and yellow ribbons.

Kate wanted to cry. *Where are you, Ben? You're going to lose out.*

Again she looked for her uncle. A group of young men stood near the entryway, but all of them were too short.

"What do I have?" called Mr. Cassel. "What lucky man gets to eat with the lady who brought this beautiful box?"

Erik's brother, John, started the bidding. "Two dollars!"

A gasp went through the audience. Two dollars? Everyone knew that was a high starting bid.

Then Kate saw her uncle, bending his head as he strolled through the outside door. She wanted to stand up and wave.

"Two twenty-five!" shouted a blond youth.

Ben glanced around, as though searching for Kate. Across the room, their gaze met, and she nodded slightly.

"Two fifty!" John called.

"Three dollars!" shouted Ben.

People laughed at the bid going so high. "Must be teacher's box," said a boy near Kate.

"Three twenty-five!" John was starting to look nervous.

"Three fifty!"

"Three seventy-five!" John brushed a hand across his forehead.

"Four dollars!" Ben's bid came strong and clear.

Oh, Ben! Kate thought. *Do you have the money to pay?*

John answered at once. "Four fifty!"

A murmur swept through the crowd, then quieted, as the auctioneer looked around. "Four fifty, I have. Four fifty for the organ fund. Do I have another bid for this big box with the big roses?"

"Five dollars!" Ben shouted.

Another murmur filled the room. Five dollars! Never before had Kate heard of a box selling for so large an amount.

The auctioneer held up his hand. "Five dollars! Five dollars I have for this lovely box and the lovely lady who made it!"

He paused, his gaze sweeping the room. John Lundgren looked down at his hands. No other bid filled the silence.

"Five dollars once, five dollars twice—sold to the highest bidder, the tall young man near the door!"

As Ben strolled forward to claim the box, a roar of applause swept through the room.

"Who-eee!" shouted someone from the back. "Hope she's worth it!" Laughter rippled through the classroom.

Ben winked at Kate, and suddenly she felt scared. *I hope so, too,* she thought. *What if I'm wrong?*

Just then the auctioneer lifted another box—a box covered with yellow ribbons.

Seeing it, Kate felt sick. *What if Ben pays all that money and doesn't get to eat with Miss Sundquist?*

11

Strange Warning

C'mon, Kate," Josie said when the last box was sold. "We're supposed to pour coffee."

But Kate refused to move until she saw what happened to Ben. He stood at one side of the room, looking around. A troubled frown darkened his eyes.

Kate felt as if she could read his thoughts. Almost every man had found the owner of the box on which he'd bid. But where was Miss Sundquist?

Over in a corner, a woman with light brown hair sat with her back to the room. From where Kate stood, she looked like the teacher.

As Kate started in that direction, she tried to catch Ben's attention. The box on which he'd bid seemed small in his large hands. And now, a married woman followed by four children was weaving through the crowd, heading his way.

Oh, Ben! Kate groaned. *What have I done to you?*

As her tall uncle caught sight of the woman, he seemed to brace himself. Beads of perspiration broke out on his forehead.

Three feet away from Ben, the woman stopped. A short man with thinning hair stood up. Ben sagged against the wall.

Again Kate looked around. This time she saw Miss Sundquist coming from the girls' cloakroom. As she sat down with Ben, the teacher's cheeks were pink, and her eyes sparkled. Only then did Kate go for the coffeepot.

Off and on, she watched what was happening. Once she saw Ben take a piece of chicken from the box. Soon after, Miss Sundquist laughed at something he said.

"I helped Ben," Kate said softly when she joined Anders and Erik. She didn't say how afraid she'd been that she'd given the wrong help.

Her brother's grin stretched from ear to ear. "He and teacher are sure having a good time."

Erik stiffened. "One meal at a box social doesn't mean they'll get married."

His words reminded Kate of Erik's brother John. She tossed her long hair over her shoulder. "Well, I hope they do. I'm on Ben's side."

"And I'm on John's." Without another word, Erik walked away. As Kate watched him go, she wished she had held her tongue.

When everyone finished eating, there were games. Then one man played a banjo. Another drew the bow of a fiddle across the smooth side of a handsaw. Kate's heart leaped with the high sweet music. She wanted to sing.

If we get an organ, I can play for everyone. I can help Miss Sundquist when she teaches us songs. Maybe I really will become a great organist.

Then the music stopped, and Miss Sundquist stood up. "We have good news. With what we've already saved, we have enough money to buy an organ."

Everyone cheered, and the teacher waited until they were quiet again. "The school board and I want to thank you for your generous help."

As Miss Sundquist looked toward Ben, he grinned. But John Lundgren turned away.

By the time Kate, Anders, and Erik left the school, the wind had grown cold. A thin coat of ice had formed on the log across the creek. As though sorry for the words between them, Erik reached back to help Kate.

When she hesitated, Erik looked straight into her eyes. "I haven't changed my mind," he said. "But maybe we should leave things up to teacher and John and Ben."

Kate felt relieved. She cared about Erik too much to have a fight between them. "Thanks," she said softly and took his hand.

A moment later, Kate felt glad she had. Halfway across the log, she slipped and almost fell. Without Erik's help she would have lost her balance.

When they reached the top of the steep hill, Anders turned around. From the edge of the ridge, the three looked down.

"Let's see if we can find out what's going on around here," Anders said quietly. But what did he hope to see?

Far below, the schoolhouse windows glowed with kerosene lamps. A cluster of people stood on the porch, then disappeared behind the building. When they came out on the road that passed the school, Kate could see them again. Their dark shapes separated, moving in two directions.

As one lamp after another went out, the light in the school grew dim. Finally, only blackness remained, and Kate, Anders, and Erik stood alone, high on the hill.

In the crisp springtime air, the stars seemed only a few feet above their heads. Below them, the trees cast dark shadows— shadows that lengthened on the hillside. Even then, Erik and Anders stood motionless, each with his back against a tree.

When Kate started to speak, Erik whispered, "Shhhhh!" He tipped his head toward a smaller tree. Kate caught his warning and stepped close to the trunk.

In the cold wind, the minutes stretched long. Then from the left a thin black shadow slipped down the hill. Slender and short, the shadow moved quickly. As it crept from tree to tree, it seemed to wait, as if listening.

When the shadow crossed the log bridge, Anders moved away from his tree. This time Kate gave the warning. Off on her right, the shadow of a larger man started down the hill. When he reached the bottom, Kate stepped forward.

Erik put out his hand to stop her. "Where are you going?" he asked softly.

"To follow them. To see what they're doing."

"No," Erik said, and Kate knew there would be no argument. "We don't know who they are. It's too dangerous."

For a while longer they waited, hoping to see more. Finally they had to give up.

As they again started for home, Kate felt disappointed. They still didn't understand what was going on around the school. How did all the mysterious pieces fit together?

When they reached Windy Hill Farm, Kate and Anders told Papa about the men they'd seen on the hill. "You're sure they didn't attend the box social?" he asked.

Anders shook his head. "They came from the wrong direction, but it was something more—something I can't explain."

"It was the way they crept around the woods," Kate said. "They acted as if they didn't want to be seen."

———

At breakfast the following Monday morning, Ben made an announcement. "I'm not going to school anymore."

"You're not?" Kate asked. "Why?"

Anders stared at Ben. "Are you crazy?"

But Tina clapped her hands. "You can play with me all day!"

The tall young Swede grinned and pulled Tina's pigtail. As quickly as it appeared, his grin faded.

"Oh, Ben!" Mama exclaimed. "You *need* to go. You need to know how to write English."

"I will learn without school," he answered.

"You could learn so much faster if Miss Sundquist helped you."

A shadow passed over Ben's face. "Yah, that is true, but I will not go."

Papa set down his coffee cup. "The ground is still too wet for planting."

"Then I will study at home till you need me," Ben answered.

"But don't you like going to school?" Mama asked.

"Yah, I like it. But I will not go." Pushing back his chair, Ben stood up, as though unwilling to answer any more questions.

As Kate walked with Anders and Lars to school, she missed Ben. All the past week he had seemed to enjoy classes, even though the children stared at him. He'd made a joke of his great height, as if it didn't bother him. Why had he decided to stop now?

When Kate entered the classroom, she felt a buzz of excitement. Everyone was talking about the box social and the money it raised.

A group of girls surrounded Maybelle. Her soft skin and auburn hair looked even more beautiful than usual. "When the organ comes, I can play it for all of you," she said.

As usual, Maybelle's voice dripped honey, but Kate felt as if an arrow had pierced her heart.

"You can?" asked one of the younger girls.

"Certainly," Maybelle answered, sounding as though everyone would be greatly honored by her playing. "I play very well."

"Just like she does everything else," Josie said softly, looking at Kate. But Kate tried to ignore the hurt she felt.

When Miss Sundquist took attendance, she looked back to where Ben usually sat. She put a mark in her book, then made an announcement.

"Those of you who weren't at the box social have no doubt heard the good news. Many who bid for the boxes were very generous."

Again Miss Sundquist glanced toward the back of the room. Quickly she looked away, as though hoping no one would notice.

"Counting the money from the social, we have over 24 dollars. On Saturday night we thought that would be enough. But the freight for shipping the organ from Chicago is going to be more than we expected. When we order, Sears Roebuck wants us to send the full amount."

A murmur of disappointment swept around the room.

"We need a total of $25.85," Miss Sundquist said. "That means we're 98 cents short. I'll talk to the school board to see what we should do."

86

Kate sighed. They were so close to getting the organ. Yet 98 cents was a lot of money. What if they couldn't buy the organ now, after all?

During the morning Kate hurried through her work, then asked if she and Erik could study together.

When Erik sat down in the other half of Kate's big desk, the younger children snickered. Maybelle's dark brown eyes looked angry. She kept watching them, but Kate paid no attention.

Erik had the book with the Morse code. "You write," he whispered. "I'll tell you what to put down."

Kate pulled out the piece of paper on which she'd already written. First she and Erik decided on a way to call each of their names. Then they went on to the other signals. *Meet me at the fork in the trail. Meet me at school.*

"Let's use the international SOS for our danger signal," Erik said. "Three dots, three dashes, three dots."

SOS   wrote Kate.   ... — — — ...

"There're two more we could use," she said as she looked at the international Morse code. Carefully she added to the list.

Understand   . — .

Wait   . — ...

By the time Erik returned to his seat, they had all the signals they needed. Kate copied off a set for Erik, and another for Anders.

As she started memorizing the signals, Kate's thoughts went back to the organ. There were 58 students in the room. What if each of them brought one or two pennies? They could take a collection and surprise Miss Sundquist.

Kate glanced around. Many of the children came from large families. For them two cents would be two pennies multiplied by the number of children in the family. That could mean twelve or fourteen cents. Too much, Kate knew.

But what if everyone brought what they could? She herself

had eight cents carefully hidden away. If they all worked together, would they have enough?

During noon hour, Kate talked to Erik.

"Great!" he said. "I'll ask the boys."

Kate talked to the girls. All of them seemed to like the idea—all of them except Maybelle. When Kate spoke to her, the other girl did not answer. A strange look passed over her face, then was gone.

Seeing Maybelle's expression, Kate felt uneasy. Something was wrong. Something more than usual, that is. Was Maybelle angry about Kate's friendship with Erik? Or even jealous?

Kate didn't know. She couldn't explain the feeling she had, not even to herself. Yet a strange warning seemed to squeeze her heart.

12

Batter Up!

$\mathcal{A}$s soon as Kate got home from school, she ran up to her room. She untied the sock in which she kept her money and counted out the coins. Six, seven, eight!

Holding the money in her hand, Kate thought about how hard she'd worked to earn that much. Every day for a week she had helped a neighbor make rag rugs.

Again Kate counted the pennies one by one, then dropped them back into the sock.

Anders doesn't have any money, she thought. *Neither does Lars.* And Ben? He had spent his last nickel at the box social.

When Kate went downstairs, Mama asked, "Why don't you give the baby a bath?"

Water was heating at the back of the cookstove. Kate poured the steaming water into a large tin basin on the kitchen table. Then she added cold water from a covered pail.

When the bath water felt lukewarm, Kate laid a towel on the table. Each time she undressed little Bernie, she felt as if she were playing with a doll. Yet this was much better. Bernie wiggled and made all kinds of funny faces. Seeming happy to be free of clothes, he waved his pink little arms and legs.

Five-year-old Tina pushed over a kitchen chair. She climbed up and knelt so close that Kate could barely move.

"Why does Bernie swing his arms so much?" Tina asked.

"He's saying hello to you," Kate told her.

The little girl was learning more English all the time. Now she stroked the baby's head. The thick blond hair lay flat as she smoothed it, then sprung back up. "How come his hair bounces?"

Asking one question after another, Tina barely waited for the answers.

With her hand under the baby's neck and his body under her arm, Kate leaned forward to wash Bernie's head. It seemed hard to believe that only a few weeks before she'd desperately wanted a baby girl.

For half a second Tina was quiet while she watched. Then she reached out. Cupping water in her hand, she scooped it over Bernie's body. "Why does he have a button belly?"

Kate laughed. "You mean a belly button?"

As Tina nodded, her white-blond pigtails bobbed up and down.

That night Kate lay awake for a long time. In her mind she went up and down the rows of desks, trying to guess how much each child could give. Every time Kate added it up, the amount fell short.

In the morning Kate took out her savings again. Much as she wanted the organ, it was hard giving the money away.

Once more, Kate counted the coins, then tied them into her handkerchief. Slowly she put the handkerchief deep within a pocket of her dress.

When Kate reached school, she stayed in the cloakroom with the pint fruit jar she'd brought from home. One after another, the girls dropped their money into the jar. Each time a coin clanked against the glass, Kate felt good.

Maybelle was the last to come in. Without saying hello to

Kate, she set her lunch pail on one of the shelves, then started to leave.

Thinking Maybelle had forgotten about the money, Kate asked, "Would you like to give to the organ?"

Maybelle lifted her chin. "Of course not!" She flounced out of the room.

Kate stared after her. How did Maybelle always manage to get the best of her?

When the warning bell rang, Kate counted the money the other girls had given. Forty-nine cents. That was good, Kate knew. But was it enough?

Outside the cloakroom, she met Erik. "How much did you get?" she asked. Erik had collected from the boys.

"Forty-two cents. How about you?"

Kate hesitated. *Forty-nine plus forty-two equals ninety-one cents. It's not enough.* But if she gave her eight pennies, they would be one cent over!

Kate slipped her hand into her pocket and felt the coins hidden there. "Fifty-seven cents," she answered.

Erik grinned. "You did it!"

"*We* did it!" Kate said, and wished she could feel as happy as Erik looked. Something still bothered her. *Even though Maybelle didn't give a cent, she'll get to play the organ.*

Yet what if they had to wait still longer to buy one? Before she could change her mind, Kate untied her handkerchief and added her coins to the rest of the money.

"You give it to teacher," she told Erik.

He shook his head. "It was your idea."

But Kate insisted. The fun of collecting the money was gone, spoiled by Maybelle.

When all the children were in their seats, Erik walked up to Miss Sundquist's desk. "We have a surprise for you," he said and set down the glass jar. "We collected money for the organ."

"Enough to pay the freight?" Miss Sundquist was surprised all right.

Erik nodded. "It was Kate's idea." He poured out the money on the teacher's desk. Together they counted it.

When they finished, the teacher's face shone with gratitude. "Exactly 99 cents—one penny over what we need! Tonight I'll send in the order."

As everyone clapped, the boys in the back row cheered. For the first time since giving the money, Kate felt happy about it.

"Thank you," Miss Sundquist said. "Thank you, every one of you."

Kate glanced toward Maybelle. The other girl smiled and nodded, as though accepting the teacher's thanks. Instantly Kate's good feelings vanished.

Miss Sundquist emptied the coins into an envelope and placed it inside her desk drawer. Then the students stood for the pledge of allegiance.

The morning passed quickly. At noon Kate ate her sandwich, then hurried outdoors. The day had grown warm, and many of the boys hadn't bothered with jackets. They were choosing sides for baseball.

Anders was one captain, Erik the other. He had already picked Lars.

"I want to play," Kate said.

"Aw, Kate," Anders complained. "Girls don't play baseball with boys."

"Yes, they do."

Her brother shook his head. "Not at school."

Kate flung her braid over her shoulder. Last spring she had been too new at school to dare insist on it. "I played baseball in Minneapolis, and you know it!"

Anders hooted. "Having a girl on a team is bad luck."

"Bad luck 'cause we'd lose!" another boy called out.

"I'm a better player than most boys!"

Anders laughed. "Sure," he said. "Just like I'm President Roosevelt."

He went back to choosing his side. "Pete!"

Erik looked up and down the line of boys, as if it was hard making up his mind. "Kate!" he shouted.

Unable to hold back her grin, she stepped forward. But Anders and his teammates booed. Never before had a girl been allowed to play.

The baseball diamond lay in the small area along the east side of the school. Next to third base, a steep hill dropped away to the muddy road. Small pieces of wood marked the bases and home plate.

As the players took their position, more and more girls came out of the school. When they lined up along the building, Kate guessed they were there to cheer for her.

Seeing them, Anders scowled. His team was up first.

Erik took the pitcher's mound. The first player on Anders' team struck out, then the second.

As Anders came up to bat, Miss Sundquist followed the girls onto the playground. On the porch behind her stood Maybelle.

Anders hit a line drive. The first baseman caught the ball, then fumbled it. He recovered in time to get Anders out, retiring the side.

When the teams changed positions for the next inning, Kate ran into school for her sweater. Though the sun was shining, the wind felt sharp. When she came back outside, Anders was on the pitcher's mound.

Back and forth, throughout the noon hour, one team took the lead, then the other. Time was running out when Anders' team led by one run.

In the bottom half of the inning, Lars was up first and made it to second base. Then Erik came to bat. The boys on the other team stepped back. More than once, Erik's hit had crossed the road into the brush on the other side.

He connected with the first pitch, but at the last minute bunted. With an easy run Erik rounded first base.

Kate was up next. As she walked to the plate, she felt glad her skirt wasn't long like Mama's. For the first time, the girls clapped and cheered.

"You show 'em, Kate!" Josie shouted.

From the mound Anders scowled at Kate. He'd give her his fastest pitch, she felt sure.

When it came, it was low. Kate stepped away from the plate, and Erik stole second base.

The next pitch was high. Kate let it go by. With Lars on third and Erik on second, they would win if she could bring them in.

"What's the matter? Scared of the ball?" a boy yelled.

The third pitch was wide, and Kate held her swing. Anders could put it right over the plate, and she knew it.

"Chicken, chicken!" another boy called.

"That's the trouble playing with girls!"

"Give me a pitcher who can get it over the plate!" Kate shouted back. She couldn't think of anything worse than striking out. Anders would never let her live it down.

Her brother's next pitch came right across, and Kate hit a foul ball that the first baseman caught on the second bounce.

"Lookee, lookee, watch that little girl hit!" someone shouted.

Kate's muscles tensed. She'd hit all right. She'd fool them all.

From along the wall the girls cheered. "Yay, Kate!"

On the pitcher's mound, Anders played with the ball, tossing it back and forth in his bare hands. Kate grasped the bat.

The next pitch came over the plate, and she swung, hitting a ground ball between Anders and third base. As it rolled over the bank into the road, Kate headed for first.

She heard a cheer. Lars had scored! The teams were tied!

Kate rounded first and kept going. As she reached second, she heard another cheer and risked a glance. Erik had made it home!

Kate started for third just as the fielder scrambled up the muddy bank, ball in hand. As Kate returned to second, the school bell rang, ending the game. Erik's team had won!

"Yay, Kate!" he called, and his teammates joined in. The girls went wild, cheering and clapping as if they'd never stop.

Kate turned toward the school with hands clasped above her head. Victory could not have been sweeter.

Just then Maybelle came out on the porch and stood behind Miss Sundquist. As Kate looked her way, Maybelle mouthed the word, "Tomboy!"

Pretending not to see, Kate glanced away. Not for anything would she let Maybelle spoil this moment of victory.

When lunch hour came to an end, the teams filed into school. The girls lined up to hug Kate.

One of the boys poked Anders. "You just gave her an easy pitch, didn't you?"

As her brother looked toward Kate, she felt sure he'd make a joke of it. Instead, he shook his head. "No, I didn't," he said, with respect in his eyes.

Filled with the warm glow of winning, Kate slid into her desk. The whole school knew she could bat as well as any boy—better, in fact, than many. Even Anders admitted he hadn't helped her out.

Then she caught Maybelle watching her. Kate flipped her long braid over her shoulder. As far as she was concerned, Maybelle didn't matter anymore. Kate didn't care what the other girl thought, nor even what she said.

At the front of the room, Miss Sundquist was taking one thing after another out of her desk. After peering into the corners of the drawer, she put everything back in again. Finally she stood up and faced the class.

"The envelope with the money is no longer here." Miss Sundquist looked flushed and angry. "You all know that this is a very serious matter."

If the money was stolen, there would be no organ. *All my hard work for nothing!* thought Kate.

"I am sure that someone would like to return the money," Miss Sundquist went on. "I'll give you a few minutes to look around the room. Check your desks and the bookshelves to see if you can find the envelope."

Knowing it wouldn't be inside her desk, Kate bent down to look, simply because she'd been told to do so. Across the aisle, Josie took out her books. Behind Kate, Erik did the same.

Her worry growing, Kate pulled out her books as they were doing. If the money she'd given was gone, all her hard work was for nothing. It'd be the same as if she'd thrown her money away.

"Let me help you, Katherine," Maybelle had left her own desk and stood behind Kate.

The sweet voice grated on Kate's nerves. Before she could answer, Maybelle leaned down and took the last book from Kate's desk. Reaching far back, she pulled out an envelope.

"Oh, Katherine!" Maybelle exclaimed. No longer was her voice honey sweet. Instead, it carried to everyone who wished to listen. "What is *this*?"

Kate felt unable to believe what she was seeing. An envelope inside her desk? How did it get there?

By now Maybelle had the attention of the entire class.

"Miss Sundquist!" Maybelle called across the room. "I found this envelope in Kate's desk!"

A murmur rippled among the students. Miss Sundquist stared, surprise and shock on her face.

She thinks I stole it, Kate thought. *How can teacher possibly think I took the money?*

13

Signs of Spring

$\mathscr{K}$ate leaped out of her desk. "I didn't do it!" she said.

Slowly Miss Sundquist walked back to Maybelle, took the envelope, and opened it. When she glanced up, she looked into Kate's eyes.

In that moment the awfulness of being unjustly accused tore through Kate. Anger replaced the embarrassment she felt, flooding her entire being. When she spoke, it sounded as if she were spitting out the words. "I don't know how it got here, but I did *not* steal the money."

"Then why did you go back inside?" Maybelle asked. "All the rest of us were watching the game."

Caught off guard, Kate tried to speak, but could not. Gone was the moment of victory she had cherished. Gone was the feeling that she'd never let Maybelle hurt her again. Somehow Maybelle had managed, after all.

"You were the only one who went back in." Maybelle's voice sounded hard and convincing, like a hammer pounding against iron.

Kate felt the pounding. There was something she needed to

remember, something she had barely noticed. Yet she couldn't recall what it was. She could only say, "I went back for my sweater."

"I suppose that's why you wanted us to bring money—so you could take it!"

"That's enough, Maybelle," Miss Sundquist said. "Sit down."

Kate sat down too. But then she saw the eyes. The eyes of every student in the room looking at her. She couldn't tell which was worse—the embarrassment of being wrongly accused or her anger about it.

Even more, Kate couldn't bear the hurt and disbelief on Miss Sundquist's face. She couldn't bear the wondering.

Feeling as if she were bleeding, Kate stared back at the other students. When they failed to meet her gaze, she knew. They were wondering too.

Just before school let out, Miss Sundquist stopped at Kate's desk. Quietly she asked Kate to stay after school.

Stay after? Kate wanted to shout. *Stay after when I haven't done anything? How can you possibly believe I took the money?*

As the room emptied, Erik dropped down on the desk across the aisle. "You have to tell teacher that someone planted that envelope."

Kate's hands knotted into fists. "But I can't prove anything! Doesn't she know I wouldn't steal?"

"Maybe not. She knows you're a good student, but she doesn't know you as well as I do."

Kate's gaze met his. "What do you mean?"

"She doesn't know how you act when something goes wrong." Erik searched Kate's face, then went on. "She doesn't know you have courage."

Kate stared at him. Erik seldom talked like this. Courage? Erik thought she had courage?

Without warning, a tear slid down Kate's cheek. Hope leaped into her heart.

The next moment the feeling died, like a candle snuffed out by the wind.

"Everyone knows I was the only one who went back into the school." Kate's voice was low, filled with misery. "What can I say? That Maybelle did it? I don't even know if that's true."

"All you have to say is what you know. You know you didn't do it."

Kate wiped the tear from her cheek.

"I still think a lot of you, Kate," Erik said softly.

She blinked and almost started crying again. "Thanks," she whispered. "Thanks for believing in me."

———

Miss Sundquist surprised Kate. The teacher kept her for only a few minutes.

"I know you didn't steal the money," she said. "It will take time to find out who did. The waiting will be awful for you, but we don't have any choice."

As Kate walked home, she thought about the teacher's words. Already the waiting seemed awful. A small place deep inside hurt one moment and felt angry the next.

When Kate reached Windy Hill Farm, she went out to the barn. She found Ben in the empty stall, working on the lur.

"Well, my little Irish girl. I hear you are a good baseball player!"

So Anders or Lars had already talked to him. In spite of her misery, Kate grinned.

"Yaah." She drawled the word the way Mama did.

"Erik chose you for his side." Ben shook his head, his eyes bright with teasing. "And you helped your team win!"

Kate giggled. "I just had a lot to prove."

While she watched, Ben glued the two pieces of the lur together. Then he wrapped long strips of thin birchbark around the horn. As he twisted the strips in a spiral, he used pitch from a pine tree to hold them in place.

"Soon it will be ready for Erik to use," Ben said as he set the horn aside to let the glue dry.

Kate felt relieved that he didn't talk about the stolen money. If it was Lars who told Ben about the home run, he hadn't said everything.

On the way back to the house, Kate realized something. Always Ben had hummed as he worked. Not anymore. Not since the morning after the box social.

At supper that night Kate avoided Papa's eyes. With all her heart she hoped he wouldn't find out what happened in school. *Mama would know I didn't take the money, but would Papa?*

All evening long Kate relived the terrible moment when Maybelle pulled out the envelope. Each time her anger flared up, Kate repeated Erik's words to herself. *He believes in me!*

Just the same, when Kate went to bed, she tossed and turned. Panic added to her misery. *How can I prove I'm innocent?*

No matter how many times she asked the question, she had no answer. All she knew was that something still nagged at her mind. Something she should remember.

Some time during the night, Kate dreamed that she clutched dollar bills in her hands. When she tried to give them away, the other children backed off. They formed a circle around her and chanted in unison: "Kate O'Connell is a thief! Kate O'Connell is a thief!"

Kate woke up sobbing in her sleep. For a long time she lay awake, wondering what to do. Then she crept down to the kitchen and took Papa's big Bible from the shelf.

Back in her room again, she lit a candle. Carefully she set the holder next to the grate that let in heat from the woodstove. Kneeling on the grate, Kate opened the Bible at Genesis.

She wasn't sure what she was looking for, and skimmed over many of the pages. She knew only that she longed to have something that would tell her what to do.

Then, in the fourteenth chapter of Exodus, she found the story of the Israelites fleeing from Pharaoh, the king of Egypt. With their backs against the Red Sea, the Israelites saw their dreaded enemy, the Egyptians, coming after them. Filled with terror, the Israelites knew they had no place to go.

In spite of the awful way she felt, Kate smiled. More than

once, Maybelle had seemed a dreaded enemy.

As Kate read on, Moses spoke to the people. His words seemed to jump off the page. "Fear ye not, stand still. . . ."

Stand still? It sounded like Miss Sundquist saying, "We'll have to wait." But Kate didn't want to wait. She wanted to *do* something, to get back at Maybelle, any way she could.

"The Lord shall fight for you."

Kate stared at the verse, then memorized it. Finally she blew out the candle and crawled back into bed. As she repeated the words to herself, she fell asleep.

———

The next morning Kate waited as long as she could before going down to breakfast. She was in no mood to face Anders and his teasing. When she came into the kitchen, she found it one of those rare moments when only Papa was there.

"Good morning," Kate said, knowing it was expected of her. But her eyes shifted away from her stepfather. Right now, Kate didn't feel like talking with anyone.

At the wood cookstove she took a bowl from the warming shelf, spooned oatmeal into it, and sat down at the kitchen table. She said table grace to herself, then began eating.

Once she glanced up. Papa was pouring coffee into his saucer to cool it.

Kate kept eating as if her life depended on it. *I hope he hasn't found out what happened.*

In one way the cooked cereal tasted good this morning. In fact, it almost felt warm and comforting. At the same time, Kate didn't feel very hungry.

Papa broke the silence. "What's wrong, Kate?"

"Nothing," she said without looking up.

"Yah? Your eyes are swollen. Have you been crying?"

Kate stared at her oatmeal. She felt surprised that Papa noticed. Then she realized she shouldn't feel surprised. More than once, he had been aware of what was happening to her. Always he seemed to care.

Yet uneasiness tightened her stomach. Papa would never defend her if she did something wrong. He'd expect her to get it straightened out. But if she was *accused* of something she hadn't done, would he believe she was innocent?

"Maybe you should tell me about it," Papa said. "Maybe I can help."

But what if you think I stole the money? What if you wonder like the children in school? Kate didn't think she could handle that.

From the next room the clock ticked loud. A piece of wood fell in the cookstove, and Kate knew Papa wouldn't leave until she told him. A small part of her felt glad.

As she told the story, her words tumbled out, one on top of another. She ended by saying, "Everyone thinks I did it."

"*Everyone?*" Papa asked.

"Well, not Erik. Not Miss Sundquist. And I didn't get a chance to talk to Josie."

"Well, I don't think you did it either. In fact, I *know* you didn't steal the money."

"You *know?*" Kate asked, and Papa nodded. The hard knot inside her stomach seemed to loosen. Still she found Papa's words hard to believe.

"But you're—" Kate thought about it. "You're married to my mother."

"And you're my newest daughter," Papa said softly. "My newest, *special* daughter. But even so, I would know. You wouldn't take that money, Kate. You're not made that way."

As Kate stared at him, tears welled up in her eyes.

Papa cleared his throat. "Some of the others know that too." His voice sounded gruff. "Just wait. You'll see."

He pushed back his chair, and Kate thought he was going to leave. Instead, Papa poured another cup of coffee. "You know, I think there's more to this than you realize. From what I've learned about Maybelle, she seems like a mixed-up little girl."

"Not so little! She's taller than I am and always mean. Sometimes she even pretends she's my friend and wants me to act like she does. If I did, I'd have to be mean to all the little girls. And I couldn't play baseball!"

Papa shook his head. "A real friend won't ask you to do something that hurts you. Is there some reason why she doesn't like you?"

"Well, she likes Erik."

Papa smiled. "And Erik likes *you*."

Kate felt a hot flush creep into her cheeks. Did Erik really like her? Times like yesterday it seemed that he did. But other times he treated her like all the other girls at school. And still other times he teased her so much she couldn't stand the sight of him.

"Maybe Maybelle's trying to get even," Papa said. "Or maybe she's mean because of what you stand for."

Kate wasn't sure what Papa meant.

"You know who you are," he explained. "You know what you want out of life."

Kate nodded. That was true. She wanted to be a great organist. And lately she'd been wanting to grow up and get married and have a family.

"Maybelle's done some foolish things. But if you forgive her, maybe you can help her."

Kate sighed. "*Help* her? *Forgive* her?" She couldn't think of anything she wanted to do less. How could that possibly make things better?

Yet while Kate was upstairs in her room, dressing for school, she glanced out a window. On the lawn below she saw more robins than she could count.

"Look outside!" Kate called down the stairs.

The first robin of spring was always something to celebrate. Never before had Kate seen so many at once, all pecking away at the ground. Watching them gave her hope.

Later, as she crossed the log bridge near school, Kate hugged one thought to herself. *I'm glad I have parents who trust me.* She dreaded seeing Maybelle again, but the knot in her stomach was gone.

I'll find out who took the money, Kate promised herself. *And I'll figure out the reason for ALL the mysterious happenings around here.*

14

Pieces of the Puzzle

*T*hat morning Miss Sundquist looked toward the back of the room, marked Ben absent, then glanced away. During announcements she said, "We'll have cleanup day tomorrow. Bring your rakes and bushel baskets."

The boys cheered. Cleaning up the school grounds meant a day without classes. When they finished working, they'd play games and have a bonfire.

Later that morning Miss Sundquist gave the spelling lesson. As usual, she pronounced words for four grades at a time. When the teacher looked at a certain row, the children knew that word was theirs.

Kate wrote down the first word. As she waited for the next one, she heard a light scratching noise. Trying to decide where it came from, she glanced toward the ceiling.

For over a week, there had been no strange noises. Now Kate heard the same sound as on the day that school opened.

Twisting around, she sneaked a look at Erik. He, too, seemed to be listening.

Miss Sundquist continued pronouncing words. Then a soft thump broke the quiet. This time there was no doubt. The sound came from directly above Kate.

Looking up, she searched the tin ceiling. From the front of the room to the back she gazed, then from the left to the right.

"Katherine," Miss Sundquist said. "Are you remembering to write your words?"

Kate ducked her head. No, she wasn't. She wasn't even sure how many she'd missed.

For the rest of the lesson, she pretended that she was thinking about the spelling words. Yet the minute Miss Sundquist finished, Erik whispered close behind Kate's back.

"Curious, Kate?"

She nodded.

"Me too," Erik said softly.

Kate turned. "Do you have any ideas?"

"Well, it's not mice." Erik sounded sure of that.

Kate agreed. "But what *is* it? Let's look as soon as we can."

When the teacher let them out for lunch, Kate and Erik circled the school. Neither of them spotted anything new. Yet Kate still felt curious about the small door just below the peak of the roof.

"I'm sure that's where the noises come from," Kate said. "There has to be a way to get up there."

To be certain, Erik walked back into the woodshed. The ladder was still along the inside wall, locked in by piles of wood.

———

Thursday morning dawned bright and sunny. The temperature was the warmest it had been since the March day when Kate and Anders traveled to the St. Croix River.

As soon as Miss Sundquist dismissed the children to work outside, Erik led Kate toward the far end of the school yard, where the creek passed into swampy ground.

Anders and Josie were already there. With no door or windows on the north side of the building, it was a good place for getting out of work.

When Kate and Erik walked up, Anders was teasing Josie. Soon they started talking about the stolen money.

"Does teacher have any idea who took it?" Josie asked Kate.

"If she does, she didn't tell me. She just said, 'Wait, and we'll find out who it is.' But it's awfully hard to wait."

"Wait for what?" Maybelle asked suddenly.

Kate jumped. On the soft ground she hadn't heard the other girl come up behind her. Had Maybelle heard what she said?

Kate glanced toward Erik. He shook his head slightly, as though reading her mind and answering no. But he didn't give Maybelle a chance to talk.

Instead, he handed her his rake. "Will you help Anders and Josie a minute? I'll be right back."

Before Maybelle could answer yes or no, Erik tipped his head toward Kate, as if telling her to follow him. Then he walked quickly away.

Kate didn't need a second invitation. She left the pouting Maybelle and hurried after Erik.

Without pausing for even a second, he passed the school and dropped down the steep bank to the muddy road. Only once did he look back to make sure that Maybelle wasn't following.

"I want to show you something I found last night," he said.

Erik led Kate north, past the swampy land across from school. Kate stayed at the edge of the muddy track, walking on grass whenever possible.

Soon Erik left the road and followed a narrow trail to the shore of Spirit lake. Safely away from any bushes, the black remains of burned wood filled a small hollow. The area was still wet, as if the wood had been doused with water.

"My brother John noticed a light and thought it might be a small fire. I hurried down to see what was going on, but the fire was already out."

Kate picked up a stick. As she stirred the charred wood, she turned up the head of a fish. "Look! I bet someone caught a fish and ate it!"

"I bet you're right!" Erik exclaimed. "It's good we came back. In the dark I missed the fish head."

"It fits with the earthworms under the school," Kate said. "Something's strange around here. Really strange." Though the wind felt warm with spring, she shivered.

Erik searched again for some sign of who the fisherman might be. Then he and Kate returned to where Josie and Anders were working. Maybelle had disappeared, and Kate didn't feel sorry.

On this side of the yard, the ground dropped sharply away. Using her rake, Kate pulled leaves from the hollows between trees. Soon she had a large pile for Erik and Anders to carry to the fire.

"Hey, Kate, slow down!" Anders complained. "You're making us work too hard."

Kate laughed. It felt good just being outside. After the long winter, the sunny day warmed her heart.

Josie seemed to feel the same way. Her friend's cheek was smudged with dirt, but her eyes looked ready for fun.

Just beyond the top of the steep bank, Josie's rake struck something. As she pulled, whatever it was followed her rake through the wet leaves.

"What have you got?" Anders asked her.

Kate dropped to her knees. She'd seen a glimpse of wood. Sinking her hands into the leaves, she caught hold of something and lifted.

"A homemade ladder!" Erik exclaimed. The leaves fell away as he and Kate pulled it free.

The narrow ladder was unlike any that she had ever seen. Wild grape vines bound short strong branches to two long poles. The branches provided rungs for the ladder.

Erik looked it over. "Whoever made this didn't have any nails handy."

"And he had a hatchet, but not a saw." Anders pointed to the ends of the branches, then the ends of the poles. "He used what he could find on the ground. Or he chopped the pieces to the right size."

"How long do you think the ladder has been here?" Kate asked.

"Not very long. The wood still looks good." Her brother tested the ladder's strength.

"He went to a lot of work to make this ladder," Kate said.

"He?" Josie asked, her green eyes dark with questions.

"He," Anders said firmly. "No girl could think this one up.

Unless she's someone unusual—like Kate, for instance."

Kate glanced sideways, expecting to meet her brother's teasing glance. When she realized he was serious, it surprised her. For the second time in a few days Anders had paid her a compliment. What was wrong with him?

His next words set her feet back on the ground. "Of course, it's Kate's curiosity that usually gets her in trouble."

Kate ignored him. "The ladder is for that attic room," she said. She looked up toward the door beneath the peak of the roof.

"Let's hide it again," Erik said. "We'll keep watch to see who tries to use it."

Together they covered the ladder with leaves wet enough not to blow away. Then they raked the rest of the area. Maybe Miss Sundquist wouldn't notice that they hadn't cleaned that corner of the yard.

While pretending that she was raking, Kate moved closer to the north end of the school. Again she glanced up at the door. For only a moment she stared at the wall, judging the distance. Then she walked on, still raking.

Yet she wanted to leap with excitement. The ladder looked just the right length!

The noises, the ladder—it all fit. What was behind that door?

15

The Night's Secret

*L*et's come back tonight," Kate said when she returned to the others. "Let's see what's up there."

Minutes later, the teacher lit a match to the large pile of leaves, sticks, and brown grass the students had raked together. They all brought their lunches outside and gathered around the bonfire.

Kate dropped down on a log to eat. "You know what?" she asked Anders, Eric, and Josie. "I've been thinking."

"Thinking?" Her brother grinned. "Well, what do you know about that?"

"I've been thinking about that fish head," Kate said. "And about Josie's sandwich—how it disappeared overnight. Do you suppose there's someone around here who's hungry?"

"My dear sister, of course there's someone who's hungry. I'm hungry all the time."

Kate refused to be sidetracked. "I mean *really* hungry."

Erik's eyes looked thoughtful. "You might have something there, Kate. Let's leave some food. We'll find out."

Anders offered his lopsided grin. "Better leave it where I can find it."

Kate tossed her head. "You mean, leave it so that wild animals can't eat it, but where a hungry person finds it."

Anders groaned. "So I can't eat all my lunch."

"Nope. Only half." Kate held out the metal syrup pail in which she carried her lunch every day. "If we all give part of what we have, he'll get a good meal."

Each of them gave at least half of a sandwich. To that, Erik added a piece of cake, Anders offered Mama's good pickle, and Josie gave a cookie. Kate packed her carrot sticks and all the other food in the pail.

Replacing the metal cover with her name across the top, she pushed it down hard. That would keep the food safe from coons or dogs or mice.

For an hour after lunch everyone raked again. When all the work was done, even Miss Sundquist played prisoner's base and other games.

As all the other students started home, Anders, Erik, and Kate stayed behind to hide her lunch pail.

"After supper listen for the signal," Anders said to Erik. "This time we'll find out what's going on."

———————

When Kate got home from school, Mama was sitting in her chair feeding the baby. Kate asked about Ben. "Does he study during the day?"

Mama shook her head. "He helps Papa. And he wanders around the house, staring out the windows. I wonder what's bothering him?"

"He really liked school," Kate said. "I can't figure out what's wrong."

"Next Wednesday is his birthday. We'll have a big supper for him. Maybe that will make him feel better."

Kate doubted it. She felt concerned about Ben.

As Mama stood up, Kate took the baby. Holding him against her chest, she patted little Bernie's back until he burped.

Mama smiled. "You're getting good at that."

Kate wrapped the baby's blankets around him, then settled

herself in Mama's chair. As she rocked back and forth, Bernie's eyelids closed. Soon he drifted off to sleep.

Kate smiled down at him, but for once she wasn't thinking about the baby. Ben had spent so much money at the box social. Was he sorry that he had bid so high?

Kate didn't think so. He and Miss Sundquist seemed to have fun together. Afterward, Ben walked her home. Whatever trouble there was had started since then.

"Ben has changed since the box social," Kate said to Mama. But neither of them had any idea what was wrong.

By the time Kate laid the baby in the cradle, she had made up her mind. She headed straight for the barn. When she heard noises in the hayloft, she climbed up and watched her uncle throw down hay for the cows.

"Ben?" Kate asked after a time. "Don't you *want* to go to school?"

The tall Swede kept pitching hay through one of the holes to the main floor of the barn.

"You could see Miss Sundquist every day," Kate added.

"Yah," he said. But his face looked like stone.

"Then why don't you go?"

Ben started down the ladder.

Kate's voice followed him. "Are you scared of her?"

With his head and shoulders above the hole in the floor, Ben looked at Kate. "I'm not scared of her. She said the whole ca-mun—" He paused, fumbling for the word.

"Community?" Kate asked.

"Yah. The whole community will talk if they see her with me."

Kate could hardly believe Ben's words. "That doesn't sound like Miss Sundquist."

"Someone maybe tell her I was a thief in Sweden?"

Kate tried to think. Did anyone else know? Perhaps someone outside the family had said something.

"I don't know, Ben, but I doubt it," said Kate.

"Well, I will tell you something. I will *not* go back to that school!" Ben disappeared down the ladder.

"Oh, Ben." Kate followed him to the ground floor. "There might be something you don't understand."

"Yah?" Ben asked. "Maybe I understand *everything*! Who could love such a one as me? I'm a—what do you call it, a jail-bird?"

Kate giggled. The word sounded funny coming from Ben. Yet it wasn't quite true. Some time before, he had stolen money from a shopkeeper in Sweden, then run away.

When Ben shook his head sadly, Kate was sorry she laughed. "You're not a jailbird. A jailbird is someone who's been in jail. You were a thief, but you paid the money back."

"Yah." Ben looked at the dirt floor instead of her.

Kate felt curious. "Ben? What happened to you after you ran away from home?" She'd never heard the story directly from him.

"I walked over the mountains to Norway. I took a ship from Oslo."

"And came to America?"

Ben picked up a small barrel, tipped it over and sat down. "On the boat I got sick. So sick I couldn't eat. I got so weak I couldn't stand up. But here I was even sicker." Ben tapped his chest.

"Inside?" asked Kate.

"Yah. About what I did. Stealing the money. Running away. Bringing shame to the name of my good family."

"And then?" Kate sat down on a covered bin. "What did you do?"

"One day, when I didn't want to live anymore, a man talked to me. He told me I had done very wrong."

For the first time that afternoon Ben grinned. "I knew that. That is why I wanted to die. But the man talked to me about Jesus. All my life I knew about Jesus dying on the cross. But I thought I would just have fun. When I got tired of that, I'd let Him save me."

Ben's eyes turned serious. "It's not much fun being all filled up with wrong things. The man said I could tell Jesus I was sorry for my sin. I could ask Him to forgive me."

"And you did?"

Ben nodded. "Yah. Jesus forgave me. Then I asked Him to be here." Ben pointed to his chest.

"In your life?"

"Yah. That's where He's been ever since."

"Then why do you think Miss Sundquist doesn't want to be seen with you?"

Ben shrugged. "I can change on the inside. But on the outside, not everyone believes. Like not everyone believes that you didn't steal the money."

Startled, Kate stared at him. So he knew too.

"I talked to Miss Sundquist," she said, and suddenly felt very glad that she had. "She knows I didn't take the money."

"She believes *you*," Ben said. "But would she believe *me*?" He shook his head and wouldn't talk about it anymore.

After supper, Anders went outside to blow on Ben's lur. His signal to Erik sounded funny—full of blats and strange noises. But Kate could catch the message: Meet us at the fork in the trail.

Then Anders stuffed a candle and matches in his pocket. In the growing dusk he and Kate set out for Spirit Lake School.

Erik met them as they had hoped. Their signal had worked! They hurried on, wanting to use every bit of light.

When they reached the school, Erik pulled the ladder from the leaves and set it against the end of the building. Without making a sound, Anders climbed up.

On the bottom edge of the door a small handhold had been cut into the wood. Anders needed to yank more than once. When he did, the ladder began to move.

"Be careful!" Kate whispered.

As Kate steadied the ladder, Anders pulled the door again. This time, it swung back, making the hinges creak.

Anders quickly crawled into the yawning black hole. As his legs, then his feet disappeared, Kate stepped on the bottom rung. Step by step she pulled herself up.

At the top of the ladder Kate leaned forward and crawled

through the opening. Just inside the door, Anders held up the candle.

Twelve to fourteen inch log beams stretched from one end of the attic to the other. Boards of different lengths were laid across the center logs. Wherever the boards did not reach the walls, there were holes.

As Erik came up behind her, Kate moved farther into the room. Between the holes in the floor she saw tin, the ceiling of the classroom below.

"That explains the noises," Kate said. "Every little sound would come through the tin."

Above them the roof rose in a peak, then slanted down to nothing at both sides of the room. At the center, the ceiling was high enough for all of them to stand. With Anders holding out the candle, they moved away from the open door.

When they reached the far end of the attic, they found old school desks pushed off to one side. Other than that, the room seemed empty.

"There *has* to be something here!" Kate exclaimed.

"No, there doesn't," Erik said. "If there's a man using this attic, he could take everything with him when he goes."

"He could," Anders answered slowly. "But would he? Especially when he goes fishing?"

"Well, let's look," Kate said. "Let's look before he comes back."

Pushing aside all thought of the risk, Kate took the candle from Anders. Could they find something?

Holding out the light, she peered inside each desk. All of them were empty.

Anders got down on his knees. Starting at the far end of the building, he reached under the end of each board.

Erik joined him, searching the opposite side of the floor. Gradually they worked their way back toward the open door.

Suddenly the candle flickered. Kate held up her hand, shielding the flame.

The boys finished their search without finding anything. Still Kate didn't feel satisfied. There had to be something that would tell them what was going on. Yet every moment they stayed put them in further danger.

Again the candle flickered. As Kate cupped her hand around it, she had an idea.

"You looked under the ends of the boards, but not all of them are nailed down. A man could hide something in the hollow between the planks and the ceiling."

Erik grinned, and the light threw shadows across his face. While Kate held the candle, the boys searched again. One by one they lifted any loose boards they found.

Halfway across the attic, they discovered what they were looking for—a bedroll.

"We've got it!" Erik laughed softly.

As Anders started to pull out the bedroll, Kate heard a noise. Moving swiftly to the door, she listened. Yes, she was sure of it. From the road that wound past the school, someone sneezed.

Kate blew out the candle. "Shhhhh!" she whispered. But was it too late? Even such a small flame could be seen for some distance.

"The ladder!" Erik exclaimed. With one swift movement he brushed past Kate, knelt down, and tugged.

Anders helped him. Together they pulled up the ladder.

As Anders reached out again, Kate heard a cough. Her brother swung the door almost shut, leaving only a crack open. In total darkness the three waited.

A minute stretched long, seeming forever. Had the open door given them away? How far away was the person? Whoever walked on the nearby road would only have to look up.

Then Kate heard the sucking of boots in mud. She knelt down next to the door and tried to see between the crack.

Closer and closer the footsteps came, sounding clearly in the damp air. *Big boots*, Kate thought. *A man's boots*. She shivered.

Straining her eyes, she peered into the darkness. But the night held its secret.

16

The Hideaway

*W*hoever walked below made no effort to hide his movements.

It must be a large man, Kate thought. *Where have I heard those footsteps before?*

Then the night was quiet. At first Kate wondered if the man had gone. Yet that wasn't possible. No sounds—footsteps, coughs, or sneezes—had faded away in the distance.

A minute or so later, she heard another noise. The person seemed nearer. If it *was* a man, where was he now?

Kate strained to listen. Whoever it was, he seemed to cross the school yard. The brown grass of winter muffled the sound, and Kate couldn't be sure.

Then she heard an exclamation. Had the man slipped in the mud by home plate?

Again Kate waited. From somewhere near at hand she heard a deep cough. A second cough came from just below the partly open door. Kate's fingers clenched, knotting with fear.

After a while, the man blew his nose from farther away. Kate started to relax. Maybe he was leaving.

His muffled steps grew faint, could not be heard, then

sounded again. Had he circled the school?

Once more, he blew his nose, this time from directly below where Kate hid.

To her it seemed certain that the man was looking up, seeing the barely open door. Yet she had no way of knowing. Afraid he would hear even the sound of her breathing, she pressed her hands across her lips.

After a time, muffled footsteps moved on. When the man reached the road again, Kate knew by the sound of boots sucking in mud. Gradually the steps faded off in the distance.

"Let's get out of here," Kate whispered.

Erik dropped the ladder, being careful not to scrape it against the wall. One by one they crept down. Anders closed the door just the way he found it.

Together the boys hid the ladder under the leaves. Together the three crept through the darkness, over the log bridge, and home.

Only when they reached the fork in the trail did Kate dare speak. "Who is using the hideaway?" she asked. "And why?"

Even in the dim light she saw her brother shake his head. "It could be Thomas Evans. But there's something that bothers me even more."

He spoke in a hoarse whisper. "If what we heard was the man who lives there, why didn't he try to come up?"

"There must be two men," Erik said quietly. "Remember the night after the social? Do you suppose one man is looking for the other?"

"Questions, questions, questions!" Kate exclaimed. "And almost no answers!"

———

Sitting in school the next day, Kate couldn't get Ben out of her mind. Maybe, just maybe, there was something she could do to help him. But she didn't want anyone else to see her talking to Miss Sundquist.

As the other children left the classroom to eat lunch outside, Kate took her time. Soon the room was empty except for Miss

Sundquist. She was grading papers, but didn't seem to be think-ing about her work. Every now and then she stared out the window.

Slowly Kate stood up and walked to the teacher's desk. She felt scared by what she wanted to do, but knew she had to try.

"I've been wondering about your uncle," Miss Sundquist said. "Is farm work keeping him home?"

Kate knew the teacher expected her to say yes. Even boys younger than Anders and Erik dropped out of school for spring planting.

"No, Miss Sundquist," Kate answered. "Papa told Ben to come."

A faint flush colored the teacher's cheeks. "He doesn't want to be here?"

"That's what he says," Kate answered. "But I don't believe him." She spoke quickly now, afraid she'd lose her courage. "He likes it here. He wants to learn to read and write English. But there's something keeping him away. He thinks you don't want to be seen with him."

"I don't want to be *seen* with him?" Miss Sundquist looked puzzled.

"That's what he says."

"Ah." The teacher's eyes lit up. "Ben misunderstood. I told him I can't be seen in the company of one of my students. The whole community would talk."

Kate felt relieved. "That's what I thought."

Miss Sundquist smiled. "And do you have something in mind?"

"Yes, I do," Kate answered solemnly. "If Ben doesn't go to school, he isn't your student anymore. But I am, and so are Anders and Lars. You haven't called on us yet this spring."

"Hmmmm, you're right." Miss Sundquist sounded just as solemn as Kate.

"It's Ben's birthday next Wednesday," Kate said. "Could you come for supper and help us celebrate?"

"You know, that's a good idea." The teacher's lips turned up at the corners. "It's important that I visit the home of my students."

As Miss Sundquist smiled, Kate wished that Ben would tell her *his* story. Kate was pretty sure she knew what Miss Sundquist would say.

––––––––

On Monday Anders went home with Erik after school. Kate was at Windy Hill Farm when she heard the long, clear notes of a lur. She listened to the rhythm being played. It was Erik!

Da daaa. Da daaa. To someone who didn't know the code it would sound as if Erik were playing a tune. But to Kate the rhythm meant a message.

When the woods fell silent, she grinned. *Meet at the fork in the trail. Bring Wildfire.* Using Ben's lur, Kate answered, *Understand.*

In the barn she threw a blanket across Wildfire's back, then slipped on the bridle. Outside, Kate climbed up. The spirited black stepped sideways across the yard. Yet she followed Kate's direction down the steep hill to the school.

Soon the path evened out, and Kate urged the mare on. When they got to the flat ground around Rice Lake, Wildfire broke into a canter. In no time at all, they reached the fork in the trail.

The mare wanted to keep on, but Kate remembered her brother's words: "Be sure Wildfire knows who's boss, or she'll take you to the moon."

Kate pulled the horse up, then waited, listening to sounds. The springtime woods seemed alive. Over and over a bird called *fee-be, fee-be.*

As time grew long, Kate grew impatient. Where were Anders and Erik?

Wildfire moved restlessly, nosing the grass at the edge of the path. *We got here in record time,* Kate told herself. Then she noticed the sun.

Between the leafless branches, its position had changed. Kate felt sure she had waited longer than she should.

Maybe I misunderstood. The notes had been clear and easy

to follow, but a nagging thought remained. *Was I supposed to meet them at school?*

Finally Kate nudged Wildfire. The spirited black moved out, again wanting to run. Kate kept her at a walk and looked carefully from left to right, observing the woods around her.

Before long, they reached a ridge. On both sides of the trail, the ground fell away. Far below, small hollows held pools of black water. Then the ridge opened onto the backside of Spirit Lake School.

Kate stopped Wildfire for a better look down between the trees. Directly below flowed the high water of the creek. Beyond that stood the woodshed and school. Everything looked normal. Why had Erik and Anders called?

Kate slipped down from the horse. Grasping the bridle, she stood next to Wildfire's head, ready to quiet her if needed.

Again Kate waited, the mare beside her. A squirrel scampered across the hill below them, rustling the dead leaves on the ground. The wind swept between the trees, rattling dry branches.

When no one appeared in the clearing below, Kate led the mare off the path and tied her lead rope to a branch. Slowly Kate crept forward.

At the bottom of the hill she crossed the large log that spanned the creek, then hurried past the woodshed. Along the back side of the school, she stayed close to the wall, then peered around the corner.

The ladder stood against the north end of the building!

Kate looked in every direction, trying to see if anyone was watching. Then she crept forward to the ladder. Reaching up, she grasped a rung with her hands.

She was halfway up the ladder when a long clear sound broke the afternoon stillness.

The lur! Erik was playing again.

Kate listened. *Meet at the schoolhouse.*

She grinned. For once she'd gotten a head start on the boys. She'd find out for herself if the man had returned to the mysterious hideaway. There was only one problem. She had no way to tell the boys she got the message.

Kate pushed the hair out of her face and continued up the ladder. If she ran into trouble, Erik and Anders would soon be here.

17

Friend or Enemy?

*S*tanding near the top of the ladder, Kate pulled at the small handhold. For some reason the door seemed stuck.

She yanked harder. When the door opened, she swung it back. Its creaking sounded loud in the afternoon sunlight.

Kate climbed up another rung, leaned forward, and crawled into the attic. At first it seemed that nothing had changed. The huge log beams looked the same. So did the boards laid across the beams to create a loose floor. Yet the daylight helped Kate see more than she could before.

A spiderweb hung in one corner. Footsteps showed in the dust. Had the man using the hideaway seen their footprints?

Kate was almost to the place where the bedroll was hidden when a sharp bang startled her. The attic turned black like night.

Kate gulped. *It's just the door. The wind blew it shut.*

But the terrible darkness confused her. *If only I had a candle!* she thought.

She started walking, then remembered the holes in the floor. If she stepped between the log beams, she could sprain an ankle, or worse. How strong was the tin ceiling above the schoolroom? She had no idea.

Her heart thudding, Kate dropped to her hands and knees. Slowly she crawled ahead on the rough boards. A sliver pierced the palm of her hand, and she yelped.

Kate stopped, tried to pull out the sliver, but could not. Once more, she started forward. This time a sliver jabbed into her knee.

As Kate stopped a second time, fear touched her, like fingers reaching out in the dark. *Which way am I going? Toward the door, or away?*

Without a crack of light, she had no way of knowing. In the total darkness, her head seemed to spin. *I'll be locked in here forever! I'll never get out!*

Kate struggled to think. She had faced into the room, then turned partway to get better light. But what did she do when she got the slivers? There was no way to know.

Slowly Kate made a quarter turn. Reaching out, she felt firm, strong boards and crawled ahead.

The next minute the boards ended. When Kate felt beyond them, she found only space. In the dreadful darkness she must have turned too far.

Once again needing to think, Kate sat back. Just then she heard a small scratching noise. Her stomach churned as she tried to push the sound out of her mind.

A second time she heard the noise. No longer could she ignore it. It wasn't scratching. From close at hand it came. Without a doubt she knew what it was.

Then a mouse scampered across the floorboards. In the darkness Kate could not tell which way it was going.

She shuddered and stood up, ready to run. "O God, you promised to be with me! You *promised!*"

Fear turned to panic, and she tried to pray. But terror kept her from uttering a word.

In the stillness she waited, her heart pounding as she listened for the mouse. Instead, she seemed to hear a voice from deep within. *Fear not. Stand still.*

A voice? No, it was the verse she had memorized. Over and over she had repeated the words. Each time she wanted to prove she didn't take the money, she had remembered, *The Lord will fight for you. You need only to be still.*

Be still. In spite of the darkness, in spite of the mouse, Kate waited, thinking about the words.

At last she felt peaceful, unafraid, even surprised. *If I just remember God's promises, it helps!*

Then, like seeing a picture laid out before her, she recalled how the attic looked by candlelight. The loose boards had been laid all one way. The length of each board stretched from left to right.

Reaching out, Kate felt the narrow side instead. The boards would give her direction!

On her hands and knees again, Kate crawled one way, being careful so she wouldn't get more slivers. A few minutes later, she banged her head on something.

When she felt a school desk, Kate knew she had gone the wrong way. Turning around, she started back in the other direction. Before long, she reached the opposite end of the building.

Now that she was closer, she saw a tiny slit of light along one side of the door. But the door refused to open.

Kate stood up and swung back one leg, ready to kick. At the last moment she realized she might tumble out of the second story.

Instead she sat down, facing the door. Again and again she kicked hard, but the door held fast. Needing to rest, she finally gave up.

Erik, Anders, where are you? she wanted to shout.

As if in answer, Kate heard a noise outside. What was it?

Then she knew. The sound of a ladder dragged across wood. The ladder being pulled away from the wall!

Kate almost cried out, but she had no idea who had taken the ladder. If Thomas Evans had made and hidden it, the mysterious man was probably back.

In the darkness Kate waited, her ear against the door for sounds from outside. After a time of silence, she knew she could wait no longer. Already the crack of light had grown dimmer. If she lost the daylight completely, there would be no way of knowing where the door was.

Moving carefully, Kate felt around until she touched a large log beam. Holding on with both hands, she kicked even harder against the door. Suddenly it burst open.

Kate crawled to the edge of the floor and looked down. The ladder was gone, all right, and it was a long way to the ground. Still, for the few remaining minutes of light, Kate could see.

She pushed the door all the way back, trying to make sure it wouldn't close again. From the other end of the hideaway she dragged a desk. Close to the door, Kate braced it, so the desk wouldn't move.

Then she pulled off her long stockings and sweater, tied them together, and knotted them around a desk leg. Her makeshift rope wouldn't reach the ground. Yet it was long enough for her to drop down without getting hurt.

Taking a firm hold, Kate swung herself out of the opening. As she dangled in the air, she heard a sound behind her.

Who was it? Friend or enemy?

––––––––

Kate landed on the ground. On the brown grass nearby was a bedroll. Beyond that, a man with his back toward Kate was lifting the ladder out of the leaves. The elbow of his jacket was torn and dirty, as if he'd fallen on it.

When the man turned and saw Kate, he jumped. The ladder fell out of his hands.

"Why are you here?" Kate asked. At the same time she stood out of reach, ready to run to safety if needed.

Then she caught a good look at the man's face. Pale and triangular, with a broad forehead that narrowed down to a thin chin. It was the man she'd seen in the Grantsburg mill!

From beneath a dirty, bent-out-of-shape hat, his gray hair fell long and stringy, as if it had not been washed for some time.

The man stood quietly, his dark eyes studying her. "Are you Kate?" he asked.

She nodded. "And you?"

The man hesitated, then seemed to make up his mind. "Thomas Evans."

Yes, I know, thought Kate. Yet his words made the newspaper article seem real. She wished that Erik would come, or Anders, or anyone at all.

"Have you been living here?" Kate asked. She tipped her head toward the school and the half-open door of the upper floor.

The man nodded.

"Why?"

"I needed a place to stay." His voice sounded tired and old.

"Why?" Kate asked again.

"Are you the one who left me food?"

Kate felt surprised. "Why, yes. If you're the one who ate it."

A half smile lit the man's face, and the years seemed to fall away. "Thank you," he said simply.

"But why are you here?" Kate wanted to know. As she stared at Thomas, her eye caught a movement behind him—across the creek on the trail at the top of the hill.

"After I went away, I remembered I left the ladder against the wall. I came back to hide it."

Kate nodded. That was the scraping she'd heard.

"I left again. As I walked through the woods, I heard some boys coming on the trail. I stepped into the brush to hide. As they passed me, their dog barked. But one of the boys told it to be quiet."

Lutfisk! Kate thought. *He must be with Erik and Anders.*

"They were talking about a girl named Kate."

Behind Thomas, Kate glimpsed the color of Erik's jacket, blue against the dead, brown leaves on the hillside.

"They wondered where you were. And I wondered if you were the girl who left me food."

Just then Kate saw Anders start down the steep hill. Afraid that Thomas would turn to look, Kate kept her gaze on him.

"I started thinking that the ladder was in a little different position," he said, "as if someone moved it. I wondered if you were trapped in the room."

"I was," Kate said. "Thank you for coming back."

"When I found a black horse, I was sure."

The boys had disappeared, hidden in the hollow through which the creek passed. *I've got to keep Thomas talking.*

Before Kate could think of anything else to ask, Thomas turned away toward the creek. Just then the boys appeared from behind the woodshed. Thomas stepped back, as if he were going to run.

Like a shot out of a cannon, Lutfisk left Anders and streaked toward the man. When he reached Thomas, Lutfisk planted his four feet and growled.

The little man straightened, drawing himself to his full height. "Call off your dog."

"Not till I know what you're doing here," Anders answered.

"Who are you?" Thomas asked.

"Kate's brother—Anders."

Thomas turned to Erik.

"Kate's friend—Erik."

As if suddenly remembering something, the man whirled around. He stared at the school yard, then looked toward the road. When he turned back, his black eyes darted this way and that. His gaze searched the steep hill, the far reaches of the woods, the trees edging down to the swamp.

At last he spoke. "Come," he said, and Anders commanded Lutfisk to be quiet.

Thomas picked up his bedroll and led them toward the woodshed. They stayed just inside the entrance. Yet the shed hid them from anyone who might pass the school or look down from the trail above.

Even here, Thomas seemed ready to run at any sign of danger. "I am innocent," he said. "I didn't do anything wrong except take a sandwich left in the schoolhouse."

"Why don't you tell us what happened?" Erik asked.

Thomas looked relieved. "I worked in Minneapolis for a wealthy family named Kempe. I did everything that needed doing in their very large house."

Fixing things, Kate thought. *Like you fixed that bench.* The pieces of the puzzle were falling in place.

"A year ago the Kempe family wanted me to build a safe into their wall. I hid it in a room on the second floor. Yet a few weeks back, someone stole some valuable coins. While her husband was still out of town, Mrs. Kempe came home. She discovered the robbery and called me to the room where it had taken place.

" 'Thomas!' she said. 'How can you do this to us? We trusted you all these years!'

"I told her, 'I didn't do it. I'm innocent.'

"But Mrs. Kempe was so angry she sounded like a different person. 'You're the only one who knows about the safe,' she said. 'If you didn't do it, who did?' "

Thomas cleared his throat, as though even the memory of that moment hurt him. "As I wondered what to say, I looked through the doorway into a large hall. At the end of the hall was a table with a kerosene lamp. A lamp that was lit."

"So you could see into the hall?" asked Kate. "Even though it was dark?"

Thomas nodded. "Just then I remembered something. A short time before, the family hired a new butler named Arthur. That's probably not his real name. He didn't seem like a butler. But I didn't think much about it till a day when I was upstairs fixing a window."

As the sun dropped behind the steep hill, Kate leaned forward for a better look at Thomas's face. "What happened?"

"I saw Arthur looking around. I asked, 'Can I help you?' He shook his head and hurried away. But it bothered me.

"When Mrs. Kempe accused me, I remembered that day. I told her, 'You hired a new man as butler.'

"Right then a shadow fell across the wall. Someone had stepped in front of the lamp. That person was listening."

18

The Bear Den

*K*ate stepped closer to Anders and Erik. Her mouth seemed dry, yet her hands felt cold and clammy. "What did you do?"

"I ran to the hall and looked around. It was already empty. Whoever had been there was gone."

Thomas looked over his shoulder, then stepped outside. Erik followed, as though afraid the man would run away.

Kate turned to Anders. "Why did you call, telling me to come here?"

Her brother grinned. "We wanted to check out the school again. Guess you beat us to it!"

From her place near the door, Kate watched Thomas. In spite of what the newspaper said, the man seemed to be telling the truth. Again he looked around, his dark eyes searching. Then he returned to the shed.

"What did the shadow look like?" Kate asked.

"It was large, but not fat. Like a heavyset man."

"Do you know who he was?" This time it was Anders who asked.

"I think so," Thomas said. "When I went down to the kitchen, the butler came in. Arthur and I usually didn't talk much. But that night he said, 'Before you came here, you were in a bit of trouble, weren't you?' I don't know how he could possibly know."

"It was true?" Erik asked.

"When I was a young man, some friends and I got drinking and did some foolish things. I learned my lesson and haven't acted that way since."

"Did Arthur want to blackmail you?" Erik asked.

"He said, 'I must make sure Mrs. Kempe knows about it.'"

Thomas's hands trembled. "Already Mrs. Kempe had lost faith in me. What would happen with one more black mark? Long before the sun came up, I crept away."

"Were you in the back of the wagon when we came home from Grantsburg?" asked Kate.

Thomas nodded. The tired lines around his eyes seemed to deepen. "I slipped out when you stopped at the granary."

"Then you hid in our barn?" Anders asked. "And this woodshed?"

Again Thomas nodded. A discouraged shadow crossed his face. "I was leaving for good. I came back to make sure Kate was all right. I'm still going away, but I'm innocent."

Looking toward Kate, Thomas touched the brim of his old hat. "Thank you for the food." He started to leave.

"Wait!" Kate called out. "Come home with us!"

The minute she said it, she felt scared. She glanced toward the boys and found them watching her. They looked worried, as though they also wondered if they could trust Thomas.

We have to be sure, Kate thought. Thomas and the newspaper told the same story. The same, except that the paper said Thomas was guilty.

Who should we believe? wondered Kate. *Is Thomas telling the truth, or making up a story?*

Somehow Thomas's words had the ring of truth. Yet he didn't give Kate the chance to think it through. "I can't come home with you. I'd bring trouble on you."

"Trouble?" Anders asked.

"Arthur is following me. If I go to your house, he'll come there."

That would be trouble all right. Kate remembered Mama and Lars, Tina and little Bernie. Just thinking about them, Kate felt warm inside, unwilling to bring danger to them.

To make things worse, Papa and Ben were gone for two days, helping a family whose house had burned down. Men of the area had gathered to rebuild it. Erik's father and brother were also there.

But Thomas doesn't want to bring trouble to others, Kate thought. She looked at him with new respect. What was it Papa had said? "A true friend won't ask you to do something that hurts you." Though they had just met Thomas, he was more of a friend than Maybelle!

"I know," Erik said to the slender little man. "We've got a perfect place for you." Erik looked at Anders. "Don't you think so?"

Anders nodded. "Yup. It'd be safe all right."

"Where?" Kate asked.

"A bear den," Erik told her. "I found it last week."

Kate stared at him. "A bear den? Are you serious?" Long ago, before Kate moved to northwest Wisconsin, her Minneapolis friend had said there would be bears. Always Kate had dreaded the idea of seeing one. Now, here was proof!

"Sure," Erik answered. "The bear won't be in it this time of year."

"Well, what if she *is*?" Anders asked with his lopsided grin. "She'd scare the bad guy away."

"But what about Thomas?" Kate asked.

"Erik is right," Thomas answered. "The bear will be out of the den. It sounds like a good place."

He picked up his bedroll. "Let's go."

Erik led them as they hurried across the log that spanned the creek. In spite of the steepness, Erik nearly ran up the hill. With no leaves on the trees, anyone could see them from the road below.

At the top of the hill, the path took three different directions.

Erik kept straight ahead, but soon they turned again, leaving the trail.

Here beneath the trees, the ground was covered with leaves. Where the sun had dried them, they rustled with each footstep. Whenever possible, Erik kept to the other places, where leaves were still damp and soggy. In the growing dusk the others followed, making as little sound as they could.

Twice Erik turned back to Kate. The first time he pointed to a maple strangely bent out of shape. The second time he stopped near the trunk of a large red oak. As Kate stared up at the massive tree, she saw a broken-off top.

Landmarks, Kate thought. *Erik knows I'll have to find my way back.*

Just beyond, he stopped at a huge uprooted tree. The mass of dirt around the roots stood high in the air, taller than Kate. On the sheltered side of the trunk was an entrance to a hollowed-out space.

Kneeling down, Kate looked into a bedding of leaves and bark and grass. Fallen brush around the space hid it well. She never would have seen the den if Erik hadn't told her.

As Kate backed away, Thomas peered into the cavity. When he straightened again, his eyes glowed with gratitude. For the first time a quiet smile lit his face.

"Thank you!" He pumped Erik's hand.

"We'll take turns coming back," Kate whispered. "We'll bring food and blankets."

When Thomas slipped into the den, he was completely hidden from sight. Yet on the way home, Kate started wondering. What if Arthur saw them leave the schoolhouse? What if he managed to follow them through the woods? How long would Thomas be safe?

————

After dark Kate returned to the bear den. "As soon as Papa comes home, we'll figure out what to do," she promised. In the meantime, the hollowed out space offered warm, dry shelter.

The next morning Kate again started for school with coins

deep in her pocket. This time Mama had given her money.

"The organ will arrive soon," Miss Sundquist had said the day before. "I don't like to ask for any more money. But if any of your parents would like to help buy music books, I'd be grateful."

Now the teacher collected the money, put it inside an envelope and then in her desk. Watching Miss Sundquist, Kate felt as if she were reliving a nightmare. At least one hundred times she had wondered, *How can I prove I'm not a thief?*

During the sunny noon hour, Miss Sundquist and the students took their lunches outside. Sitting on a stump away from the porch, Kate kept watch on the schoolhouse door.

She was almost through eating when out of the corner of her eye she caught a movement. Slowly Kate turned her head. Along the edge of a group of girls, Maybelle crept toward the door.

Her quiet movements jogged Kate's memory. The day of the baseball game Maybelle had come out on the porch not once but twice!

Like a wave rushing toward shore, anger washed across Kate. With every part of her being, she longed to follow Maybelle, to accuse her. Yet if Kate moved too quickly, Maybelle would see her.

Even as she told herself to wait, Kate felt frantic inside. What if Maybelle again stole the money? What if she once more put it inside Kate's desk?

Then Kate saw Miss Sundquist turn her head. The teacher was also watching Maybelle. The moment she disappeared inside the school, Miss Sundquist hurried after her.

Kate followed the teacher. Without making a sound, Kate walked into the entryway just as Miss Sundquist spoke.

"Please give me the envelope, Maybelle."

As Kate edged forward, she saw the teacher halfway across the room.

"What envelope?" Maybelle asked from near the teacher's desk.

"The envelope you just put in your pocket."

Without moving, Miss Sundquist waited. Slowly Maybelle

walked over to her. Slowly she pulled out the envelope and gave it to the teacher.

"You understand how serious this is, don't you?" Miss Sundquist asked.

Maybelle lifted her chin, but lowered her gaze to the floor. "Yes, ma'am."

"You also took the other money, didn't you?"

Maybelle's gaze left the floor and shifted to the window. "I was outside during the game."

"But you went inside for a minute." Kate spoke from the doorway.

At the sound of her voice, Maybelle turned toward Kate. A flush colored Maybelle's cheeks, giving her away.

"You understand I need to clear Kate's name," the teacher said.

Maybelle's angry gaze stayed on Kate. "Yes, ma'am."

"I want you to start by asking Kate's forgiveness for what you've done to her."

Maybelle groaned.

"I'm waiting," Miss Sundquist said.

As though knowing she had no choice, Maybelle spoke. "I'm sorry, Kate." But her voice was filled with resentment.

After lunch hour, Miss Sundquist told the class that the person who stole the money had been found. Though her name was now cleared, Kate felt no joy in it. She could only feel sorry for Maybelle.

As Miss Sundquist finished speaking, a wagon pulled into the school yard.

"It's the organ!" shouted one of the girls.

In no time at all, the boys and the delivery man brought the large crate inside. Using a hammer, Erik pulled the huge wooden box apart.

When the boards fell away, the new organ stood by itself at the front of the room. Kate longed to run her hand over the solid oak finish. In the light that shone through a window the keys gleamed white.

"I think Katherine should be the first to play," Miss Sundquist said.

First to play? Kate found it hard to believe. *Play for everyone to sing?*

Feeling as if she were in a dream, Kate sat down on the wooden stool. She pumped the pedals, and the organ filled with air. As she played "The Battle Hymn of the Republic," the others joined in.

Then Erik moved up beside her. Above all the others, Kate could hear him sing.

———————

Late that afternoon, Kate pulled the weekly newspaper out of the Windy Hill mailbox. When she reached home, she spread it out on the kitchen table and searched through the news stories. Would there be anything more about Thomas?

Not until the inside pages did Kate see a small notice:

T.E. If you are somewhere in northwest Wisconsin, please return. I have wronged you. Your job is still open to you. J.K.

"T.E. ," murmured Kate. "Thomas Evans. And J.K. must be Mrs. Kempe!"

Filled with excitement, Kate hurried to the door. "I'll be right back!" she called to Mama.

Pulling on her sweater as she ran, Kate headed for the barn. *There's just enough time. I can get to Thomas and back before dark.*

Anders was nowhere in sight, but Kate felt sure he wouldn't mind if she took Wildfire. She slipped on the bridle, then led the mare outdoors to leap on her bare back.

In the quiet afternoon, Wildfire's hooves pounded against the dirt trail. Before long, the path on which Kate rode crossed another trail. As she slowed down to take the turn, Kate heard a noise that didn't seem to belong to the woods. What was it?

Stopping the mare, Kate listened. This time she heard the sound clearly—a cough from deep in a man's chest. He was not far away.

At a break in the underbrush, Kate directed Wildfire off the trail. Soon the tree limbs grew too low to ride beneath. Kate slid to the ground and led Wildfire into a clump of pines.

"Quiet, girl, quiet," she whispered in the mare's ear.

A moment later, Kate heard the cough, closer this time. Heavy boots thudded on the dirt path. Were they the boots she'd heard outside the attic hideaway? How could she see the man without being seen?

Leading Wildfire, Kate hurried over to a stump. With her hand still on the bridle, she climbed up.

As the footsteps drew close, Kate peered between the pine branches. Then she saw the man. Tall and heavyset, he wore a black coat and trousers.

She caught only a glimpse of his face, but it was enough. No wonder his boots sounded familiar! She'd heard them on the wooden sidewalk outside Unseth's drugstore!

Arthur, she thought. *It must be Arthur the butler!*

The man's footsteps faded into the distance. Kate felt relieved that he was gone. Then her heart started pounding again. Arthur was heading straight for the bear den. Thomas was in danger!

19

Trapped!

*K*ate leaped onto Wildfire's back. She pulled up the reins, then hesitated. If she rode toward Thomas, she'd catch up with Arthur. She might even lead him to Thomas's hiding place. Instead, Kate needed to find help.

As the sun slipped below the horizon, she entered the main trail. Turning Wildfire toward Windy Hill Farm, Kate nudged her into a canter. When the path opened onto a field, she flicked the reins across the mare's flank.

Wildfire broke into a gallop, and Kate felt a twinge of uneasiness. Maybe she had given her too much freedom. Yet even now Thomas might be in trouble.

Soon the mare reached the far side of the field. As she reentered the woods, Kate tried to pull her in. Instead, the left rein snapped!

Only a foot of leather dangled from the bit. For an instant Kate stared at the useless piece in her hand. Dropping it, she started tugging on the other rein.

Then she remembered. "Pull evenly," Anders had said.

But why? He had explained that too. "If you don't, you'll pull her head around too fast. She might lose her balance and fall."

With her left hand Kate clutched Wildfire's mane. Up a hill she raced, as though dogs nipped at her heels. Starting down the other side, Kate bounced up and down.

"Whoa!" she cried. But the mare ran blindly on. "Whoa!" Kate shouted again. The galloping pace pounded against her body. A new panic filled her. *I can't hang on much longer!*

She remembered the distance to the ground, the flying hooves. Then she sensed what to do. *Lean forward*. She stretched across Wildfire's neck.

Farther.

Kate squeezed her knees to keep from falling off. Edging forward still more, she strained for the broken rein. It swung loose, just out of reach.

Kate stretched again. Her bruised body cried out, but this time she grabbed the broken rein. Using every ounce of strength, she pulled the two reins, tightening the bit. Gradually the mare slowed her headlong pace.

By the time Wildfire came to a halt, Kate trembled with weakness. For a minute she sat there, trying to calm herself.

When she clucked to the horse again, Kate was still shaking. In spite of her worry about Thomas, she held Wildfire to a trot the rest of the way home. In the dusk that follows the setting sun, they entered the Windy Hill yard.

Kate found her brother inside the barn. Together they decided what to do. Anders stepped outdoors and blew an SOS on the lur. Then he and Kate hurried to the house.

When they told Mama what had happened, she shook her head. "And where is Thomas now?"

They explained about the bear den, and she smiled for the first time. "A good place," she said.

Then worry clouded her blue eyes. "It's a bad time for Papa and Ben to be gone. I wish they were here." Yet neither one would be home for another day.

Soon Erik came to the door, and Mama made a quick decision. "There's only one way Thomas will be safe. Take him to Grantsburg. Put him on the train for Minneapolis. But Anders, you must promise me one thing."

"Yes, Mama." Anders grinned, as though sure he knew what was coming.

"You and Erik take care of Kate. One of you must always be with her."

"Yes, Mama." Anders tried to keep a straight face. "I'll take good care of Kate."

"So will I." Erik looked more serious about the matter.

Anders shook his head. "It's a shame it takes two of us to keep an eye on her."

Kate opened her mouth, a quick reply on her lips. Then she caught Mama's expression. "And I'll take good care of *them*," Kate said in her sweetest voice.

Erik returned home to tell his family where he was going. On the way back he would stop at the bear den to get Thomas.

In the darkness before the moon rose, Anders and Kate hurried to the barn. Quickly they hitched up the big workhorses, Dolly and Florie. Then Anders pitched straw into the back of the wagon. To that he added two large crates.

As Kate worked, she felt the wind sweep across the hill. She and Anders were spreading blankets and canvas over the boxes when Erik suddenly appeared.

"Where's Thomas?" Kate whispered. "We're ready."

At a signal from Erik, the short, slender man ran forward. Anders lifted the canvas, and Thomas slipped into the empty space between crates. Anders pulled the canvas forward, then climbed up beside Kate and Erik.

From the high spring seat Kate glanced around. Close by, deep shadows darkened any possible hiding place. If Arthur had followed Thomas and Erik, they had no way of knowing.

Then Dolly and Florie started out of the farmyard. On the trail to the main road, Kate looked behind them more than once. Except for the wind whispering in the tall pines, everything seemed quiet.

Only when they were out in the open did Kate speak to Thomas. "I read about you in the newspaper," she said. "The woman you worked for says she's sorry. She wants you back."

Thomas raised the front of the canvas. "That may be. But if

Arthur finds me, he won't let me go back."

Before long, a half moon rose above the horizon. Trees became black outlines against the nighttime sky. In spite of the reason for their trip, Kate enjoyed sitting next to Erik. She liked having such a good friend.

Soon she turned around again. "Thomas? Did you hear anything when you were in the bear den?"

Thomas nodded. "I heard footsteps and a cough. I'm sure it was Arthur. He coughed on the train when he asked the conductor about me."

In the moonlight only Thomas's face showed. "Arthur wants to stop me from telling the truth. If he finds me, no one will believe I'm innocent."

No one? Kate remembered when she had thought the same thing about her own situation. Both Erik and Papa had encouraged her. Now Thomas needed that kind of trust.

"We believe you're innocent," Kate said quietly.

But Thomas shook his head. "Arthur is a dangerous man. He knows that I know he stole the coins. When I heard him talking, I sneaked into a freight car that was switched to the mill."

Several miles farther on, Thomas spoke again. "Maybe the message in the paper is a trick. What if I go to Minneapolis and the Kempes accuse me?"

"You have to find out," Erik answered. "You can't run away the rest of your life."

Anders glanced back. "Mama gave us money to send a telegram. What do you want to say?"

The wagon rolled on while Thomas thought. Finally he told them the message, saying *stop* where each period would be:

WILL COME BACK IF YOU CLEAR MY NAME STOP
NEED PROTECTION FROM THE REAL THIEF STOP

When they reached Grantsburg, the darkened town was quiet with sleep. Anders slowed the horses for the train station, but they found it closed.

"I'll wake up the operator and ask him to send your telegram," Anders told Thomas.

As they started past the building, Kate caught sight of a large poster. "Wait a minute!" she told Anders. When the horses came to a halt, she jumped down from the wagon.

Tacked to a wall was a large poster with Thomas's picture. WANTED, it read. THIEF OF VALUABLE COINS. In smaller letters was a description of Thomas, then the large words: REWARD OFFERED FOR RECOVERY OF COLLECTION AND INFORMATION LEADING TO ARREST OF THIEF. At the bottom was the name Stanley Kempe and a Minneapolis address.

Just seeing the poster made Kate feel sick. No doubt there were such notices all over town. Wherever Thomas showed his face, people would recognize him and believe he was guilty.

Erik joined Kate to read the poster. "We better keep Thomas hidden till we get Big Gust. Thomas doesn't need anything more right now."

When Kate and Erik climbed back on the wagon, Erik suggested that they go to the mill. "This time of year it's open all night. The men work twenty-four hours a day."

"We'll drop off Kate and Thomas," Anders said. "You can get Big Gust while I find the telegraph operator."

Erik shook his head. "I don't want to leave Kate alone. We'll stay at the mill till you come."

A long look passed between the two boys. Kate had seen that kind of signal before. Anders did not argue with Erik.

At the Hickerson Roller Mill two wagons waited outside. Anders held the horses, and Kate and Erik dropped onto the platform. The large main door was nearly closed against the chill of the night. Kate tiptoed over and peeked through the crack. As the worker pulled bags onto the scale, he whistled a tune.

Kate edged back. At a safe distance from the door, she whispered to Erik. "Let's try another way."

To the right was the office, so Kate headed toward the long storage shed on her left. Staying within the shadows, she jumped off the platform, then crept along the front of the mill.

Near one end of the shed, she found a sliding door slightly open. Pushing it wider, she slipped through.

Erik went back for Thomas. When they caught up to Kate, Erik carried a barn lantern.

By now Kate's eyes had grown used to the dimly lighted room. The floor slanted down toward the main part of the building. From near the scale, a lantern cast long shadows.

Here in the shed, sacks of grain were piled four or five high, but they offered little shelter. If they could reach the stairs and upper floors, there would be plenty of hiding places. But how could they get past the man at the scale?

For a time the three waited. Then, as though the worker heard something, he lifted his head and listened. He left the scale and headed toward the office.

"C'mon," Kate whispered. It was the chance they needed. They raced toward the room with the roller mills, then up the stairs.

At the top, darkness surrounded them. Then Kate heard the scratching of a match, and Erik lit the barn lantern.

Step by step, they tiptoed across the large second-floor room. They were near the bins and just above the scale when Kate heard someone come in.

A low voice rumbled. "I'm looking for this man."

"That's Arthur," Thomas whispered.

"Oh, yeah," another man answered. "Now that I think of it, I saw the posters around town."

"The people I work for sent me to find him," Arthur answered. "If it's all right with you, I'll take a look around."

"Sure thing. Don't want to take any chances."

From below, heavy boots thudded across the floor.

"Let's separate," Thomas whispered. "It'll be harder for him to find us."

Frantically Kate looked around. Where could she hide?

Then, near the bins, she saw a large wooden barrel with a cover. The box next to it was just the height she needed.

Kate slid back the cover, climbed onto the box, then dropped into the barrel. As she replaced the cover, she left it partway open.

"We'll keep an eye on you," Erik whispered as he blew out the lantern. Then he and Thomas vanished into the darkness.

A moment later, Kate heard heavy footsteps coming up the stairs. *Thud. Thud. Thud.* With each step the man moved closer.

20

Ben's Birthday Surprise

$\mathcal{A}$t the second floor the footsteps stopped not far from where Kate hid. For a minute or two, she heard nothing. Was Arthur listening?

After a silence, the thudding steps passed on to the next flight of stairs. Kate pushed aside the cover of the barrel and stood up. Where was Erik?

Then she remembered the Morse codes they had used on the lur. Softly she rapped the signal for Erik's name. When she heard quick raps in answer, she climbed from the barrel.

With her hands out, groping in the darkness, Kate moved in the direction of the raps. She bumped into Erik coming down a ladder close to her hiding place.

Erik lit his lantern again. They hurried through the passageway to the room with a hole in the floor.

"Where's Thomas?" Erik whispered. "Arthur must have followed us. Somehow he saw us come in."

"Wherever Thomas is, he must have a good hiding place."

"Not good enough," Erik said. "We've got to get out of here."

Kate agreed. "Arthur *knows* we're here. He won't give up till he finds us."

She started back through the passageway. In a moment Thomas was there, a black shadow scurrying down a ladder from the catwalk above. He, too, had hidden where he could watch for Kate's safety.

As Erik headed for the stairway, Kate clutched his sleeve. "Wait," she whispered. "Arthur's coming back."

The three stood motionless. Directly above them, heavy boots crossed the floor, moving toward the stairs.

"If we take the steps, we'll get caught," Thomas said.

"The rope!" Kate answered. Turning around, she dashed back to the large hole in the floor.

The minute she picked up the rope, Kate felt scared. If she slipped and fell, no soft hay would cushion her landing.

"Hang on tight!" Erik warned.

Below, Kate saw only blackness. How far away was the floor?

Erik held out the lantern to help her judge the distance. Even so, Kate dreaded dropping down. Her fingers felt stiff and clumsy on the rope.

From the stairs came the sound Kate feared. *Thud. Thud. Thud.*

"Hurry!" Erik whispered.

Kate pushed off. Into the air she swung, her muscles tight with her fear of letting go. But there was no time to waste. Arthur would find Erik and Thomas.

On the rope's second swing, Kate let down her foot and felt the floor. With a soft bump she landed, then flipped the rope in Erik's direction.

As heavy boots started toward them, Erik blew out the flame in the lantern. Seconds later Kate heard him land nearby. Then Thomas dropped, catlike, beside them. Together they melted into the darkness away from the opening.

In the next instant, the thudding boots crossed the floor just above them. *He never tries to be quiet*, Kate thought as she had before. Through the large hole, she saw light slide around the upstairs room, casting long shadows on the walls.

Next to the railing, the light stopped on Erik's lantern. Arthur reached down and felt the glass. Was it still warm from the flame?

The man straightened and held his own lantern above the hole. The light settled on the rope. Though out of his reach, the rope swung back and forth, giving them away.

Moving quickly, Arthur left the railing. His steps sounded hurried as he crossed to the stairs.

"There's a door," Erik whispered, pointing into the darkness.

He was first outside, with Thomas close behind. As Kate followed, the door slipped out of her hands. Caught in the wind, it slammed.

Kate gasped at the noise. Everything they tried seemed to leave a trail.

They had come out at the front of the building. As Kate's eyes grew used to the darkness, she saw the road and tracks. In the moonlight they offered little protection. Where could she and the others hide?

Then Kate remembered the walkway over the Wood River. "Follow me!" she cried.

Leaving the mill behind, she fled across the bridges. The water tumbled over the dams, muffling other sounds.

Beyond the river, Kate kept running. Erik and Thomas stayed with her.

Only once did Kate glance back. "Watch out for the clay pit," she told Thomas. "It's seventy feet deep!"

She raced on, her every thought focused on one question, *Where can I hide?*

Then the large rock loomed up from the darkness. Kate was panting when she reached the far side. Erik and Thomas ran beyond, toward the cars for carrying clay.

Kate dropped to the ground and tried to catch her breath. Had they managed to get away? She heard no pursuing footsteps, only the sounds of the nearby river.

As she huddled in the shadow of the rock, the minutes stretched long. *Where's Anders?* Kate wondered. *Why doesn't he come?*

Then she had a new worry. *How will he know where we are?*

Panic as real as the tumbling water washed through Kate. If Arthur followed, would the rock offer enough protection?

Kate started to stand up, ready to run again. In that instant, words slipped into her mind. *Be still* came the warning.

Through her fear, she sensed a promise. *The Lord will fight for you. You need only to be still.*

Kate crouched down, almost hugging the ground. Her heart thudding, she remained where she was.

From her hiding place she heard a dog. The barks seemed to come from beyond the dams. The sound seemed strangely familiar.

On hands and knees, Kate crept forward to see around the rock. Toward the millpond, a large shape looked black against the night sky. Then Arthur hurried off the end of the walkway. The tumbling water had muffled his footsteps!

Crawling backward, Kate stayed low, close to the rock. If she had moved, she would have run right into him!

The dog barked again, nearer this time. Could it be? Was it possible Lutfisk had followed them to town?

Then a man's voice rumbled in the darkness. "Come out, Thomas. I know that you're here."

No! Kate wanted to shout. *Don't do it!* Instead, she had a strange thought. *It's up to Thomas now.*

As she listened, Kate heard a growl she would recognize anywhere. From near at hand it came, from deep in Lutfisk's throat.

Sudden footsteps pounded the earth. Running hard, Arthur passed the rock where Kate hid.

"Stop!" The cry pierced the night.

A shadow moved quickly. "Arthur, stop! There's a big hole! You'll get hurt!"

Arthur's steps slowed, but he was running too fast.

The shadow stretched out its arms. Thomas, standing between Arthur and the clay pit!

Arthur crashed into Thomas, knocking the smaller man to the ground. Arms and legs sprawled in every direction.

A second later, Lutfisk caught up. Standing above the men,

he growled. Thomas and Arthur stopped their struggling, lay
still.

Turning, Lutfisk barked in the direction of the walkway. Arthur started to move, but Lutfisk growled again.

Thomas raised his head. "Kate! Call off your dog!"

"Lutfisk!" she commanded, and he obeyed her. As she held
him, the two men stood up.

Thomas faced Arthur. "I've been running from you long
enough." His fear seemed to be gone. "I've got something to tell
you."

"I've got something to tell *you*," Arthur answered. "Mr.
Kempe wants me to bring you back."

Thomas straightened to his full height. "I suppose you convinced him that I stole the coins."

"No, just the opposite. When Mr. Kempe got home, he found
the bag where I had hidden them. He knew I had taken the
coins."

Thomas stared, disbelief on his face. "You're making things
up."

Arthur shook his head. "No, I'm telling the truth. Mr. Kempe
said he'd forgive me. He'd give me a second chance to work for
him. But only on one condition. I have to bring you back."

"Sure!" Thomas's laugh sounded hard and brittle. "You're
still a liar. I should have let you fall in the pit!"

"The pit?"

In the light of the moon Thomas nodded. "Erik tells me it's
seventy feet deep."

Arthur stepped back, as if afraid that even yet he could tumble in. "Thanks," he said. "But I still need to explain. Mr. Kempe
told me, 'Find Thomas. Bring him back, so his life isn't ruined.
If you don't, we'll turn you over to the police.' "

"Police? That's us!" Big Gust's deep voice leaped ahead of
him. When he reached Arthur, the marshall stood more than a
foot and a half taller than the other man.

With Big Gust was Charlie Saunders, the county sheriff.
When they heard Arthur's story, Charlie said, "Well, let's check
it out. If you're telling the truth, you won't mind if I telegraph

Stanley Kempe. We'll know right away if it's safe for Thomas to go home with you."

While the four men went to the telegraph office, Kate and the boys waited in the firehall where Big Gust lived. The sun had been up for some time when the village marshall arrived with Thomas.

Big Gust asked Kate and Anders and Erik to explain everything that had happened. When Kate told her part of the story, she ended by saying, "I was going to run. But I remembered a verse about being still."

Big Gust smiled. "I want to show you something." From his desk he picked up a small Bible—a New Testament. On the last page he pointed to carefully written words.

"I can't read Swedish," Kate said.

A teasing grin lit the marshall's eyes. "Well, I can. I wrote this."

Then he looked as serious as Kate had ever seen him. "It says, 'Anyone who reads these verses will be much benefited by them.'"

"That's it!" Kate said, grateful that Gust understood what she meant. "I stayed close to the rock and was safe."

"And now all we need is to hear from Mr. Kempe," Big Gust answered.

Just then a knock sounded on the door. "Thomas Evans?" a young man asked. He held out a telegram.

With shaking fingers Thomas tore open the envelope. He read the message aloud:

WE HAVE PROOF YOU ARE INNOCENT STOP
WE ARE SORRY FOR ALL THAT HAS HAPPENED STOP
WE WOULD LIKE TO HAVE YOU COME BACK STOP
THIS IS YOUR HOME STOP
THE KEMPE FAMILY STOP

Anders and Erik cheered, but Kate watched Thomas. After all her trouble with Maybelle, she thought she knew how Thomas felt.

A few minutes later, Arthur and the sheriff brought a second telegram. Big Gust read it aloud.

ARTHUR IS TELLING THE TRUTH STOP

Shortly before noon Kate and the boys walked with Thomas to the train station. Arthur stood off to one side, waiting for the train to come in.

When the long whistle sounded, Thomas thanked Kate for everything she had done, then turned to Anders and Erik and did the same. "All this time I was running away. And I didn't even need to be afraid!"

Thomas shook his head, as though still not believing how everything had worked out.

"I will never forget all of you," he said as he told them goodby. "Thank you for believing in me." The look in his eyes said even more than his words.

As the two men stepped onto the train, Thomas turned back for a final wave.

———

On the way home Kate remembered. "Tonight is Ben's birthday supper!"

When they reached the Windy Hill mailbox, she pulled out a letter from Sweden. "It's from Mama's parents. I hope it isn't bad news." She pushed the letter into a pocket for safekeeping.

While Anders and Erik put the horses in the barn, Kate hurried to the house. She found Mama swirling frosting on a chocolate layer cake.

Her mother sighed. "I'd forgotten how much time things take with a baby!"

"I helped you!" Tina said.

Mama smiled. "Yah, you're a good big sister." Yet as she pushed the hair out of her eyes, Mama looked nervous.

Kate poked her head through the dining room doorway. The large clock seemed to tick faster than usual. Soon Miss Sundquist would be here, and there was still plenty to do.

"I'll set the table," Kate said quickly.

When she finished, Mama checked what Kate had done.

"You have one more place than we need."

Kate grinned. "I forgot to tell you. I invited Miss Sundquist for supper."

"Forgot?" This time Mama's smile was real. She laughed out loud. "That's probably just what my little brother—my *big* brother—needs!"

From then on, Mama hummed as she worked. When Ben came in from outside, she told him to clean up for his birthday supper. Ben winked at Kate, but followed Mama's orders.

Moments later, Kate whispered the secret to Papa. Even Anders slicked back his thatch of blond hair.

The family was gathered in the kitchen, almost ready to sit down, when a knock sounded at the back door.

"I'll get it!" Kate said.

"Ben's closer," Mama answered. "Let him."

As Ben opened the door, he stepped back in surprise. Miss Sundquist stood there in a coat and dress she had never worn to school. On her head was a large hat with silk flowers.

"*God dag*, Ben." She smiled up at the tall young man.

Ben blinked, surprised by the Swedish greeting. His answer seemed stuck in his throat.

"Happy birthday, Ben," the teacher said.

This time he managed a grin. He stretched out his hand as though telling her to come inside.

Then Mama took over. She led the family into the dining room and seated Ben and Miss Sundquist across from each other. Tina sat next to Ben, and Lars next to Miss Sundquist. Erik found a chair beside Anders.

When Kate brought in the baked chicken, she served it first to the teacher. Ben took his usual big helpings, but seemed embarrassed. Yet as the meal went on, he started talking about Sweden. Each time the teacher laughed, Ben's gaze met hers across the table.

As soon as Kate finished serving, she sat down. For the first time she saw what Tina was doing. Like a door opening and closing, the little girl's head swung back and forth. First her gaze clung to Ben's face. Then her bright eyes watched the teacher.

Finally Tina laid a hand on Ben's sleeve. In a clear voice and her best English, she asked, "Ben, do you and Miss Sundquist love each other?"

Mama gasped. "Tina!"

Ben's face turned red. Miss Sundquist flushed pink. She stared at her plate, as though it were the most important piece of china in the world.

Ben was the first to recover. He grinned down at Tina. "Miss Sundquist and I just need time to find out."

Ben's voice was quiet, but Kate knew he wanted the others to hear. The teacher's face grew even more pink, but she no longer stared at her plate. When Ben looked her way, she was watching him.

After Ben blew out the candles on his cake, he opened his presents. There was only one that really mattered—the gift from Miss Sundquist. On a sheet of paper the teacher had written three columns of often-used words. First came a Swedish word, next its English translation, then how the English was pronounced.

"I thought you might need a tutor," the teacher said softly. "Someone to help you study English at home."

"I need a tutor very much," Ben answered. Across the table they smiled at each other.

Only then did Kate remember the letter in her pocket. When Mama opened the envelope, Kate saw the letter was a short one. Mama read aloud, translating for Kate:

Dear Ingrid,
   For many years we have wanted to set our eyes on you once more. We have wanted to know your daughter Kate.

Mama looked up, and Kate felt the warmth of being loved. She had never met even one of her grandparents, but Grandma and Grandpa wanted to know *her*!

Then Mama continued reading:

   Now we would have another privilege to meet your husband Carl and Anders and Lars and Tina. But there's something more.

*We have learned that when Ben ran away, he went over
the mountains to Norway. From there he sailed to America.
When he sent money to repay the shopkeeper, Ben said he
planned to go to Minnesota.*

*We have purchased tickets for the next ship. If we come
to your farm, will you help us look for Ben? We do not want
to die without finding him and making things right between
us. We want to tell him that we love him still.*

"Oh!" Mama exclaimed. Tears streamed down her cheeks.
"After all these years, to think I will see my parents again! But
it's such a long boat trip for people their age. Can they get here
safely?"

"They can, Ingrid," Papa said. "We will pray."

And it's a long train ride, Kate thought. *Halfway across America. What if they get lost?*

Then Kate remembered her baby brother. "Do Grandpa and
Grandma know that Bernie's been born?"

Mama shook her head. "They'll have an even bigger surprise,
finding Ben here!" For once she didn't try to wipe her tears away.

As if just understanding the letter, Ben stared at Mama.
"They want to make things right with *me*?"

Never before had Kate seen the tall young man with wet eyes.
Deep inside, she felt the surprise of it.

Then her mind leaped ahead. How soon would Mama's parents step off the train? No longer would they be just a name at
the end of a letter. *For the first time, I'll really have grandparents!*

Kate looked around the table. "I wonder what Grandpa and
Grandma will think of all of us." *I wonder what they'll think of
Miss Sundquist. And Erik.*

"They'll like us," Mama said.

Kate believed her.

Acknowledgments

Every now and then, while researching a book, I stumble across something I know about but never expect to see. One of those moments occurred while visiting The Depot, the St. Louis County Historical Society Museum in Duluth, Minnesota. There, in the J. C. Ryan Logging Room, I found "Kate's organ."

Closed, the organ looks like a wooden suitcase, complete with carrying handle. Then Maryanne Norton, assistant director of the museum, opened the "suitcase" for me. As the lid came up, a small pump organ folded out, complete with keyboard and pedals. In earlier times, such organs provided music when traveling preachers visited lumbering camps.

Gus Clark and his Dells Mill Museum at Augusta, Wisconsin, gave me another real-life experience—the opportunity of seeing a mill operate as in the early 1900s. Judy Pearson and Clarence Wagman offered further insights about the Jacobson Mill on the Wood River and the Hickerson Roller Mill in Grantsburg.

With every book in this series, I have turned to one couple, Walter and Ella Johnson. Once again, I offer my deeply felt thanks for their careful response to questions, their memory for detail, their giving of time, and their strong sense of story.

Diane Brask's experience with a runaway mare inspired a slightly different version with Kate and Wildfire. Over the years,

Diane has also answered my great number of questions about horses.

Wallace Early and Alton Jensen helped with a variety of details, while Gary Nelson sparked my interest in the brick factory's clay pit. Wade Brask and Ronald Schulz gave special assistance with the Spirit Lake School. Mildred Hedlund and Eunice Kanne's book, *Big Gust: Grantsburg's Legendary Giant*, provided details about Big Gust.

Sandy Fulton offered her musical wisdom and research. Robert W. Nelson shared his experience with the *lur*, his understanding of Swedish ways, and his recommendation of Kerstin Brorson's book *Sing the Cows Home*.

I'm grateful to Roger Inouye and Elaine Roub for their special encouragement while I was writing this book. Charette Barta, Doris Holmlund, Jerry Foley, Penelope Stokes, and Terry White gave valuable suggestions for the manuscript. My thanks, also, to the entire Bethany House team.

Finally, I owe yet another debt to two special people—my husband Roy and my editor Ron Klug. Both have shown unusual understanding of Kate, Anders, Erik, and the rest of the Windy Hill folk. Our conversations go beyond the story line and "Who can do what?" to "What would happen in real life?" They help me believe that somewhere along the way, my characters have become people.